FIRE HEART

FIRE HEART

JOYCE CH'NG

Snowy Wings
PUBLISHING

TURNER, OREGON

For my family.

CHAPTER I

IT WAS SAID THAT the first sword maker was female. That was why all swordsmiths were women, as respected as the war chieftains and members of the Council. The Goddess of Swords shaped the first blade in eight days, thus forming the week of work, and rest—for she rested on the eighth day.

Lunes t'Ulan, the greatest swordsmith, made the Moonlight sword when she was in travail and remained hard at work even when the midwife urged her to stop. She brought forth her daughter the moment the Moonlight blade was sharpened and blessed with the blood from the birthing process.

Her daughter was, of course, Yin t'Idan, the swordsmith who created the Council sword, wielded by the Bearer at the start of every Council meeting. The swordsmith lineage went down several paths and deviated into different cadet branches, each with their own style, their own philosophy, their own colors.

When Wehia Jirin t'Doniyat arrived at the t'Tolani

holding, it was the swordsmith lineage and shared kinship she had in mind. Scruffy because of the long journey, from her minor holding in the fens, to the City, Wehia wished only for a place to cool her feet and warm her empty stomach. On her back was strapped her family heirloom, the blade she called Cold Steel.

What would Mistress t'Tolani say when she saw a slight figure, dust-covered and wearing dun-brown travel clothes, at her door? And what would the forge mistress say about the t'Doniyat, the makers of ornamental and kitchen knives and daggers?

"Better to say that you are a maker of ceremonial knives and daggers than a maker of kitchen utensils," her mother, Rohana t'Doniyat, had said, washing her hands in a basin, her work apron smeared with polishing oils. "Kitchen knives, *pfffft*."

"I want to learn how to make a full blade," Wehia had found herself saying. Her mother eyed her like a fen falcon pinning down a rice-field mouse. "I am of age now and I am ready."

"I hope it's not just an impulse and you really want to make a sword. Making a sword is a long process, Wehia!" Rohana frowned, making her look even fiercer.

"Yes, I know, Mother. I am ready to learn to make one!" Wehia insisted.

Rohana sighed. "You need to have a better understanding of sword-making and its demands. The techniques you have learned here do not necessarily carry over. Well, if you are so adamant about it, go to the t'Tolani holding, to my cousin's household. She will teach you. Go to the City, open your eyes a bit, broaden your horizons. Perhaps you will attain full status as a forge woman there as well."

Wehia blinked—the t'Tolani! The holding, which was in the City of Swords, was famous for its exquisite blades. They made blades for the blood families, the aristocrats who ran the land. Her mother had never before mentioned that the t'Doniyat and t'Tolani were kin. Wehia was amazed that she was related to such talented forge women.

"Yes, Hadana t'Tolani is my cousin," her mother said. "Now, go wash your hands. You have to polish the dagger for Lord Furego's wedding."

Wehia curbed her rising excitement and obeyed.

And so it was decided that Wehia would seek apprenticeship with the t'Tolani. Word was sent ahead and, on the dawn of fourteenth day of the Sickle Month, the girl donned stout walking boots and warm clothes, bade farewell to her mother, and began her journey to the City of Swords.

It would take her about two eight-days to get to Fen Gorr, the town where the ferry docked, leaving for the City twice a day. The ferry was not the most direct method of travel to the City, but it was acknowledged to be the easiest and safest. The alternate route that wove through unforgiving marshland was best avoided by those unfamiliar with the area.

"The way through the marsh may seem shorter, but it is a nasty, wet journey and you would have to hire a guide or risk getting lost," said Wehia's mother. "Besides, traveling by ferry is the traditional route for Shrine pilgrims."

"But—" Wehia opened her mouth but decided to shut it again.

She was impatient and anxious to get to the City in time for the week of Novice-Taking but had to admit that the prospect of journeying through marshland did not tempt her. She was not confident on horseback, so that was not an option. She just had to take the longer route.

This was Wehia's first time walking to Fen Gorr and she was naturally anxious. Brigands were common in this part of the fens, even with soldiers on horseback patrolling the area. Furthermore, border people were said to rob travelers. Unlike brigands, border people were landless and ever drifting. They existed, miserably, in filthy encampments along the edges of the fens, but most were itinerant. Wehia knew—had been told, time and time again by her mother and her aunts and the forge women—that they were trouble but pitied them nevertheless. How could she not? They led wretched lives, begging, even stealing livestock to survive. At times, they would set fire to tracts of fen land. The patrols were supposed to keep them in check too.

Wehia, despite the sympathy she felt, refused to take any chances. She avoided the parts of the fen where the border people were known to loiter.

Her nights were spent in small village inns and cheaper travelers houses, where the accommodation was shared, six travelers to a room, on one's own mat. The problem was not knowing whether one would survive the night without being robbed, or worse! Wehia slept with her money next to her skin and her sword by her side, but she could not rest easy and found herself exhausted and groggy on the days following such nights. Still, the weather held up, she encountered no dangers and experienced no mishaps, and Wehia managed to keep up a reasonably brisk pace, arriving at Fen Gorr in the afternoon of the fifteenth day of her journey.

Wehia took the midnight ferry, and in the mid-afternoon the next day, was both thrilled and relieved to see the soaring spires and towers across the water as the ferry neared its destination. This was her first time in the City of Swords and she could hardly believe the crowds of people everywhere, the noise and the smells and the sights. It was all a blur and Wehia felt momentarily overwhelmed as she stepped off the boat. But no, she must not waste precious time, and she must not let her mother down! Following the street signs, she squeezed her way through the throngs of people walking along the River Verru, feeling dwarfed by the steam exhaust chimneys, statues, and buildings that rose all around her.

She experienced a surge of awe when she saw the Council Hall, with its white, marble dome, a magnificent basilica that stood in the center of the City. The afternoon sun had gilded the dome with gold. The beauty took Wehia's breath away. She praised the Sword Goddess silently when she passed the Shrine crowded with pilgrims and devotees. A road connected the Council Hall to the Shrine buildings like an important artery to the heart. From the Shrine, the roads and streets grew narrower, leading to lanes, alleyways, and canals. After some searching, she found the blue tradesman's door of the t'Tolani holding.

Wehia lifted her gloved right hand and tugged at the bell pull, using the code taught by her mother: a kin-code, their own language.

A minute later, the door opened. A serving woman in blue greeted her politely, with a slight bow, and ushered Wehia inside, through a warm courtyard, surrounded by walls covered with a lush lacery of green leaves and brown branches, and into a small hallway, out of which two arched doorways opened, one in the facing wall, and the other to the left.

"Please wait here. Mistress Hadana will see you shortly," the serving woman said, bowing once more and retreating through the front archway.

Wehia waited impatiently, twirling the edge of her tunic with her fingers. Before too long, a tall woman with red hair strode through the archway. She was dressed in a simple robe of sky-blue, the color of the t'Tolani, the water-steel people, and wore an imperious, impatient expression. She was accompanied by a girl about Wehia's age dressed in a clean, blue smock, her hair brassy gold, framing a heart-shaped face.

"Wehia Jirin t'Doniyat? I just received word two days ago that I should expect you," said the woman. "I am Mistress Hadana t'Tolani. You are welcome. Geri will show you to your room."

Hadana t'Tolani then turned on her heel and disappeared back through the archway.

The girl, Geri, nodded and smiled. "Good day," she said. "Will you follow me, please?"

She led Wehia through the archway on the left and into a wide, open space in the center of which rose a spiral staircase.

"Our sleeping quarters are above," said Geri, who gestured for Wehia to follow her. They proceeded upwards, passing two levels. At the third, Geri led Wehia down a corridor to her bedroom.

"Mistress Hadana thought you would feel more comfortable in your own space." Geri opened a polished wooden door and stepped back to allow Wehia to enter.

Dropping her bag, Wehia looked around her. Although spartanly furnished with a clean, white bed and a wooden table on which sat a bowl of gleaming fruit, it was larger than her own room back home. On the table were a plate of cheese slices and a loaf of fresh bread. Wehia's stomach rumbled.

"Here's the ablution room," Geri said, opening another smaller door through which Wehia saw a basin, a tub, and a rack. "And this is your cabinet." Geri indicated a compact wooden box in the corner of the room. "You can put all your belongings in it." The box's lid bore the crest of the t'Tolani: a singing crane, wings spread in flight.

"Your day will start tomorrow at dawn," Geri continued. She hesitated and then added, "Do not mind my aunt. She is a woman of few words and can seem stern, but she is also kind, in her own way."

"You are my cousin, many branches removed," Wehia said.

"Yes, indeed. Well, I will be back to take you to the dining hall for the evening meal." And with that, Geri withdrew from the room.

Famished, Wehia ate the bread and cheese, noting how fresh the food was. When she was full, she washed her face in the ablution room, delighted by the feel of the cold, crystal-clear water. The tub was made of brass and was bowl-shaped, fitted with taps, levers, and pipes. She tested the levers to see if they were working. Hot and cold water. And clean. So clean. She bathed quickly, washing away the travel dust.

Refreshed, Wehia Jirin t'Doniyat, the daughter of Rohana t'Doniyat, drew Cold Steel from her scabbard. Light shimmered along the slim blade. She went through the Figure-Eight drill to while her time away before Geri came back to fetch her for the evening meal. She itched to explore the t'Tolani holding. However, with her belly satisfied, she was suddenly overcome with exhaustion and, when Geri came to take her for the household's evening meal, she found Wehia fast asleep.

Geri watched the girl for a moment and then gently shook her awake. Rubbing sleep from her eyes, Wehia followed her young t'Tolani kin to the dining hall.

CHAPTER 2

FOR A WEEK, Wehia Jirin t'Doniyat fetched water from the spring duct located next to the t'Tolani forge. The spring ran quick and hissed like sea spray. It was also skin-numbingly icy. Wehia climbed the slight hill leading to the duct, lowered the bucket into the water and filled it, then made the journey down the hill. The forge women were demanding, always testing the apprentices. They wanted their water replenished immediately. Wehia endured. It was the same at all swordsmith holdings: Apprentices fetched water. They were *expected* to do so, even when there was already available hot and cold running water. It was part of training and she shouldn't complain. She had done the same at her own holding's modest forge.

Her thighs hurt from the constant climbing. Her arm twitched from carrying the heavy buckets. When she spilled any water in the forge, the women reprimanded her for her carelessness. She endured any scolding silently. She bit down her responses, lowered her head, and carried on with her chores. When she finally sank into her bed at day's end, she hurt all over. Cold Steel in her hands was a blessing.

Despite the hardship, Wehia was grateful to be so close to the blade-making, the roar of the fires, the clang of hammers coming down hard on anvils, the smell of coal dust and sweaty women clad in forge leather. Her being thrilled to the sound of burning steel lowered into water and the sight of the huge steam cloud it made. The t'Tolani used some of the finest steel. The Council sword that stood in the august Council Hall had been made by their ancestress, Yin t'Idan. The sword was a symbol of impartiality, as well as unity between blood and swordsmith holdings. Their lineage was as bright as unsullied silver. The blades they made deserved only the best.

Wehia hardly spoke to her aunt, Hadana t'Tolani. As Mistress of the Holding and the forge, she was busy with commissions and offers. For days, while she worked on a longsword destined for the hands of Princess Madan, the ruler of the Outer Marshes, Aunt Hadana was curt, almost to the point of rudeness. Really, her attention was focused on the sword so that she barely noticed her surroundings. Geri Shaara t'Dora *ef* t'Tolani bustled about, running errands for the forge women. She wore the dark blue of a senior apprentice (she told Wehia that she had only recently achieved this status), her hair tied up into a bristly ponytail. In the light of the forge, the shiny strands looked like thin brass shavings. She often spared some thought for Wehia, sharing bread and minced-fowl soup from the holding's kitchen. Once the midday meal was over, Geri would disappear into the forge to aid one of the women while Wehia struggled with the heavy ladle used for scooping water at the spring duct. Once more, the shouting would begin, the sounds of vigorous industry pounding at her ears. Wehia watched and worked, ignored by the rest of the t'Tolani women.

"You have to endure this," Geri said to Wehia one day as they sat having their evening meal. By then, Wehia was feeling painfully isolated, out of place in the strange forge of arrogant women. She wanted to pack her bags and go home, back to the kind and compassionate holding where she belonged.

"I remember the same kind of treatment for . . . oh, at least eight eight-days—"

"Eight weeks? Two months?" Wehia grimaced.

"Yes, two months—when I began my apprenticeship," Geri continued. "They didn't spare me, either! I cried myself to sleep for weeks. It will get better. I promise."

Wehia nodded and ate her stew. Perhaps it would get better. She held on fervently to that hope.

The following eight-day, Wehia fetched water from the spring duct, and also began to carry lumps of iron ore from the storerooms. Again, she endured, because it was apprentice work, as Geri had said. Her mother got her ore from the bog down their holding's path and harvesting at that holding was also left to the apprentices and daughters. It was dirty work, with the harvesters stripped to their loincloths, their faces covered with cloth masks. Carrying ore from the t'Tolani storerooms was easier but still messy. Wehia ached all over. The skin on her hands blistered.

Her muscles were sore. At day's end, she held Cold Steel and practiced, only to wince at the flare of pain along her arms and legs. She sat down and traced the barking-dog crest and style-mark on the blade. Her dreams that night were of sleek, brown ore dogs chasing her along the bog.

The third eight-day saw her fetching water from the spring duct, carrying lumps of ore from the stalls, and sweeping the floor of the forge at day's end. Wehia quelled the spark of rebellion in her chest, as it was apprentice work, and she knew her aunt was testing her. A daughter of a swordsmith holding that only fashioned kitchen knives was unworthy. She gritted her teeth and persisted.

The fourth eight-day saw her fetching water from the spring duct, carrying lumps of ore from the storerooms, sweeping the floor of the forge at day's end, and washing the ladles. Wehia's tears tasted bitter in her mouth. She longed to knock over the buckets of water and scream her frustration, never mind the consequences. She'd had enough. She was just too exhausted to care. She even stopped practicing with Cold Steel at the end of the day.

Wehia felt as if living at the t'Tolani's holding were a farce. She was being tolerated, like a pesky fly hovering over the kitchen pots. At best, she was cheap labor. At worst, she was considered a joke, a subject of ridicule at the forge women's dinner table.

Wehia t'Doniyat had had more than enough. It had been more than a month since she had left home and she wasn't progressing as quickly as she'd first thought she would. It was already the Axe, the beginning of harvest time. The Stolati hummers, their colors shimmering like the most cherished gems, were darting about the fig trees and the courtyard, sipping the fig juice with their long tongues. Wehia couldn't appreciate their beauty. She was too angry. She wanted to speak her mind to Hadana.

She found her aunt at the forge. The woman had a cloth mask covering her nose and mouth. She was pouring glowing cast iron into a crucible.

"Dear Aunt Hadana," Wehia began tentatively.

"Not now," the muffled voice said, bearing a hint of irritation in it. "Can't you see I am busy, child?"

Wehia t'Doniyat bristled instantly. She was seventeen, at the cusp of adulthood. She had journeyed alone to the City and fought off shifty pilgrims with her sword—she was not a child!

"Aunt Haldana, I have to speak, for I can bear it no longer."

Blunt as all swordsmiths were, blunt were her words. Hadana t'Tolani straightened her back. She was a tall, imposing woman. The orange fires of the furnaces outlined her and gave her a sun's corona, as if she were Lunes t'Ulan herself or even the Goddess of Swords. Wehia stood her ground, remembering the stance her sword mistress had taught her. All the power in her belly, radiating to the Earth, and the Earth giving her the power she needed.

Hadana pulled down her mask. She had thin lips, a broad, slightly hooked nose, and eyes of dark amber. Wehia thought she looked like a warrior queen. "Speak quickly," said the older woman. "The work will not wait for anyone."

The forge fell silent. Wehia ignored the lump in her throat. She had to speak. Her heart pounded. "Aunt

Hadana, I have spent four eight-days fetching water, carrying ore, sweeping the forge, and washing the crucibles. I long for actual smith work, Aunt. I want to start my apprenticeship."

Hadana stared at her for a while. Wehia felt as if she had grown an extra head or a limb. Then, Hadana began to laugh, and the laughter echoed in the large forge. The rest of the forge women joined her and the sound mocked Wehia.

"You, a child of a holding that makes dinner knives? You want to learn from the purest of the swordsmith holdings? *Ha!*" Hadana said, her eyes bright. Wehia flinched at her aunt's words, but Hadana was right. The t'Doniyat were deemed worse than unworthy. Why had Mother even asked her to seek her apprenticeship under the t'Tolani? Did she think Wehia deserved to endure such abuse from a kinswoman? It wasn't right!

"Your hands touch sullied ore. Your blades are not good enough as gifts to the lords and ladies of the Council. Why do I have to teach you?" Hadana's words made Wehia cringe.

"Because I want to make a full blade!" Wehia blurted out. Her voice bounced and echoed off the walls of the forge. "Because I love the sword! I love the blade!"

One of the forge women barked out a sharp yelp of mockery. "Loving the blade is not enough! Go back to your holding, ore dog child!"

"Do you want to fight me?" Wehia challenged the woman angrily. The forge woman cackled aloud.

Hadana glared at her forge woman with the ferocity of a blizzard. "Cease your unnecessary insults!" she roared. "And you"—to Wehia—"do not challenge my forge woman. Bear in mind, *child*—I have the power to refuse your apprenticeship."

The words made Wehia stop. She still shook from head to toe, trying very hard to keep her temper under control. How rude the t'Tolani were to call her an "ore dog," how immensely arrogant! Why had her mother even recommended this poor excuse for a holding? Just because they were the purest lineage didn't make them good people. Her head spun with the insults. Her heart burned. Regret felt hollow in her stomach. She shouldn't have bartered away her precious daggers and made this futile journey.

"Ore dogs help us find our ore," she said through clenched teeth. She would leave. *She would leave this ridiculous excuse of a holding.* "They are my holding's symbol, our family crest, but we are not dogs. Judge us by the quality of our blades. We are the t'Doniyat, makers of ornamental daggers and kitchen knives, and we are proud of our work!"

Hadana gave her a long, hard look. Finally, she said,

"Another twelve eight-days. Then, I will give you my answer." She pulled up her mask and went back to the crucible, cursing softly under her breath.

The forge women laughed and went back to their tasks, while Wehia t'Doniyat clenched and unclenched her hands. Three more months.

Three more months.

CHAPTER 3

WHEN THE GODDESS OF SWORDS held the first blade in Her hands, She announced it was done and She was pleased. When She was done resting on the eighth day, She rolled up Her sleeves and went back to shaping the world. With Her first blade, She carved out the months of planting and sowing, harvesting, wintering, and planning. Men and women held shovels, hammers, and sickles so that their fields were ready for the seeds to grow and last year's weeds removed. When the fruits hung heavily from the branches and the animals fattened for the markets, it was for the dagger, scythe, and flint. The air turned cold and breath plumed white when people sharpened their swords, readying their knives and sabers with the whetstones, for brigands sometimes used winter to enrich their pockets, despite the efforts of vigilant policing by blood-family soldiers. It was also the last of the hunting, so that game would hang from the larder's rafters.

Wehia Jirin t'Doniyat marked the eight-days on her

sparse room's wall with a piece of charcoal. At night, rebellion roiled in her chest. Unable to give her unhappiness voice, she swung Cold Steel in the beautiful Figure-Eight drill she had been taught and drew strength from the memory of its naming ceremony.

"I name thee Cold Steel
May your will twine with my will,
May your song ring true,
sharp like the Goddess's wit and strong like Her arms.
May you come to no harm.
May you come to no harm."

Her sword held above her, Wehia had stood before the burning censer of t'Doniyat bronze, the intense fragrance of Three Queens incense filling her nostrils and wreathing her with smoke. Six of the t'Doniyat holding's most senior women stood behind her, three to her right, three to her left, each woman with a slender, brown-orange-coated ore dog beside her. Wehia's mother, who led the ceremony, beamed as she blessed her daughter and the sword. The forge women then placed their right hands on Wehia's back to signify their approval of the naming, and Wehia shivered in her white robe, feeling the sword come alive in her hands, like a gentle pulsing along the blade, self-conscious at how childish the naming poem sounded. Cold Steel's original name had been lost for a long time. Nobody knew what it was. Her great-grandmother had taken it to her grave. The maker's mark on the blade didn't divulge any secrets, either. So, renaming her, giving her a new name, had felt right for Wehia. The naming ceremony had lifted her spirits and made her one with the sword.

At the t'Tolani holding, she nursed the memories, polished them, and whetted them until they were singing softly, keen-edged.

She was kept working at the forge and endured the mocking eyes of the watching t'Tolani forge women. She fetched the spring water from the hill, carried the ore from the stalls, swept the floor of the forge, and made sure that the crucibles and ladles were washed clean. By the time the forge women had emerged from their rooms, the forge was ready for use. She woke before the strike of the first gong, even before the kitchen started stoking its fires for the day's work. Wehia focused all her attention on her tasks. Her mother had taught her that: sharp, cold focus, like a knife. That was how she had made her first dagger, a commissioned gift for a minor lord from a fen holding. She remembered the days and nights of hammering, folding the steel until it had been tough and whetting its edge until it had gleamed in the forge's light.

That was about the same time she had found Cold Steel. Wehia had been exploring the holding's attic and armory, drawn by promise of adventure and sheer curiosity, the mystery of the place—nobody ever spoke about the armory.

Those were bright memories, precious and secret.

They kept her strong.

In the early hours of the day, when the morning was still night, Wehia Jirin t'Doniyat would open her window and gaze out into the City, at the imposing dome of the basilica and the towers that stood, one at each of the basilica's four corners, like silent sentinels.

Her room was quiet, as it stood at the end of the corridor. Wehia imagined the t'Tolani holding, a broad and tall building, with a spiral stairway at its center, as resembling the inside of the pink conch shell she had discovered once along the bog shoreline. Sometime during its journey, the shell had cracked, revealing the spiral. On the tip of this building roared the signal fire. All swordsmith holdings had them. They could send messages by changing the colors of the fire. The women tending the fire were taught the different kinds of powders and hues. Blue was for an ordinary message, green meant peace, and red danger. For long-distance messages, they used signal flares with bow and arrow as well as messengers who traveled on foot and horseback.

Wehia was glad for the quiet. It gave her the opportunity to listen to the City. The brass clanks of pistons, bells, and horns. The cries of nighttime hawkers and vendors selling their goods. The soft murmurs of people still walking the streets at night. She loved the sight of fires lit on roofs. These soothed her, just as practicing with Cold Steel did.

Geri Shaara was proving a friend. The girl would pass her parcels of food—fen rice wrapped in lotus leaf; grilled fish stuffed with fragrant herbs; fresh, crisp, fragrant bread full of nuts and seeds; hot morani stew in a sturdy wooden mug. They didn't have much time to talk. The forge was suddenly inundated with commissions since it was close to the Feast of the Flint, and all senior apprentices, like Geri, were kept busy, either wrapping the completed blades in the finest spider silk or preparing scarlet scabbards for their mistresses.

Wehia was gratified by Geri's food parcels but wondered at her kindness. They had spent some nights, before the busy weeks had arrived, talking about their holdings, about their personal likes and dislikes, and their hobbies. Geri loved daggers and practiced with them. Wehia enjoyed listening to the girl's stories about the t'Tolani household, even about Hadana, which made her stern aunt seem less intimidating. Geri spoke about her mother who had passed away from an illness when she'd been just a child. She still missed her very much and envied Wehia's closeness to her own mother, as the t'Doniyat girl often talked about Rohana during their chats.

Geri's kindness, her openness, and the intimacy between them warmed Wehia's heart. It was the only bright thing in her life at the time. Everything was so grim in the forge. And she still felt like an outsider.

"When I feel sad, I count my blessings," Geri said. "I have my aunts, my cousins, the forge, a warm bed to sleep in, and food to eat."

"Hmm . . . I wish it were that easy for me . . ."

"Are you saying I'm a simpleton?" Geri prodded Wehia's arm, giggling.

"No! Of course not!" Wehia felt her face flush.

"It *is* that simple for me. I don't ask for more," said Geri. Her smile lightened Wehia's heart.

"It's good to remember the good things," she added. "It will help you feel better."

It was four days before the end of the Scythe Month, before the Feast of the Flint, when the hides of livestock were ready for skinning and their flesh for waxing. There was suddenly a commotion in the forge, with much laughter and drumming. The forge women had taken out frame drums and were beating a pattern of sounds. Wehia recognized it, just as she recognized the many kin codes of the swordsmith holdings. It was a song of celebration for the end of an important commission. Her own holding's women played the same tune, but with some tonal differences. The frame drums were light, the goatskin stretched. They were the size of straw rice sifters back home.

As Wehia watched breathlessly, Hadana t'Tolani entered, looking like a queen councilor. She wore a shimmering, blue gown with silver embroidery at the hem, silver vines curling up the skirt to the waist in a fine and delicate design. Her red hair was braided and wrapped around her head and, cradled in her arms as if it were a sleeping child, was a scabbarded longsword, almost the length of a grown man.

There was a flare of light, the nostril-piercing smell-burst of coppery Three Queens incense, and the forge women ululated with joy, their frame drums vibrating and glowing, their hands a blur, their mouths wide open, tongues moving rapidly.

With surprising tenderness, as if she nursed a sick child, Hadana t'Tolani slid the sword out from her crimson sheath with a click and a soft sigh, almost an exhalation, of metal. Wehia's heart leaped in her throat, for it was a glorious sword, shining like the brightest of stars. The sword seemed to contain all the shades of the sea, from the deepest of greens to the lightest blues.

Hadana began to dance with it, effortlessly twirling the sword around, mouthing soundless words to its flight of Figure-Eights: swordswoman and sword, in perfect harmony. Wehia swore the sword had a song, and that she sang proudly like a newborn sun. It had life, just like Cold Steel. All swords had lives of their own. This one sang as if she bore the stars in her steel . . .

I am alive! I am alive! I am alive! I am a star that shines!

Wehia's heart overflowed with joy. She wept and vowed she would make a blade like that one day.

CHAPTER 4

GERI GAVE WEHIA a plate of freshly-grilled sausages. The fragrance of oil and sizzling fat made Wehia's mouth water. The City called it "first sausages," the produce of the farms and fens exactly an eight-day after the Feast of the Flint. Where she was born, it was just Celebration, or Celebration of the Flint. It was simply a time for feasting, to enjoy the land's bounty, and to prepare for the winter.

The sausages were a perfect golden-brown, the edges of the skin darkened by fire. She could see the distinct grill marks across the glossy skin, which had been made from the animal's intestine. Wehia cut through a sausage, revealing dense blood and meat, with bits of juicy fat. She had never before had sausages filled with blood, their taste all copper and minerals. She was surprised she liked it. The sausages made at home were sweeter and lightly glazed with maltose honey. They were delicious and loved by all in her holding.

Wehia was so grateful for Geri's company. Of all the senior apprentices and daughters of the t'Tolani holding,

Geri was the only one who bothered to talk to the lonely t'Doniyat girl. Nobody wanted to be associated with a child from a lowly swordsmith holding that only made kitchen knives. Word was also going around that the t'Doniyat made forks and spoons too . . . such low-quality fare, such unworthy craft. Wehia was furious, unable to counter such thinking, lest she lose her apprenticeship. It was not true that they made forks and spoons, but there were swordsmith holdings that made kitchen utensils for their livelihood. Didn't people use these utensils when they ate? Wehia believed that each holding had their own particular purpose—a gift, so to speak. Making kitchen utensils was not dishonorable. Why did the people of some holdings feel that they were superior to others?

Three more eight-days and she would hold Hadana t'Tolani to her promise.

One afternoon, a group of men called at the holding and were received in the main hall. The guests were treated to freshly-grilled sausages and hot fen tea. The household servant who had served the refreshments could not resist stopping by the forge to gossip about the handsome lord and his grand entourage, as well as their fine clothes and the trays of elaborately wrapped gifts they had brought with them. Geri's name floated in the air and caught

Wehia's attention. She was surprised. Why was Geri receiving these obviously important guests with Hadana? Was a sword being commissioned? Was Geri going to have a hand in making it?

Later, at their evening meal, the t'Tolani apprentice confirmed that the men had come to discuss sword and dagger designs, but she merely shrugged when asked if she would be working on any of the commissioned weapons. Geri seemed distracted and unusually quiet.

"Are you all right?" asked Wehia.

"I'm just tired," replied Geri. She excused herself soon after the meal, saying she had a headache and needed to sleep.

Wehia would have dearly welcomed an early night too, but she still had chores to complete. She sighed as she made her way back to the forge. The guests and their finery were soon forgotten.

One eight-day before Hadana gave her answer.

With a sigh that came from the depths of her stomach, Wehia finished stacking a pile of ore-rocks, her hands sore, despite being gloved. The work was exhausting and her back screamed for a warm compress, or a long, uninterrupted soak in her tub. She was the last one in the forge, yet soft sounds pinged in the silence—

the creak of the metal crucibles settling, the whisper of wind sliding across the floor.

A sound alerted her. Someone had walked into the forge. The footsteps were light, like a swordswoman's. Wehia looked up.

It was Hadana t'Tolani. She wore leather, the type swordswomen wore when they were practicing. Her right hand held an exquisite sword, complete with silver filigree for the cross guard. It was a working sword that had seen actual combat—the blade had tiny nicks along its edges. Imperiously, Hadana stood before Wehia. "Fight me," she ordered.

Wehia stood up on suddenly-watery legs. Her voice shook. "I do not have my sword with me."

"Get it."

It was a command, and Wehia immediately obeyed. She flew up the stairs, dodging corners, startling the odd forge woman she met on the way to her room. She ignored all the curses flung at her, running up the spiral stairway. She grabbed Cold Steel, slammed the door, and ran down the stairs again, only to slow to a walk, controlling her breathing. Hadana would rather see her niece overly-excited and panting; it would be a swift way to defeat her. Instead, Wehia t'Doniyat steeled her heart, recalling the calming exercises her sword mistress had taught her, and walked sedately back to the forge. *"Still your heart. Do not be impulsive,"* her sword teacher had often warned. *"Listen to yourself!"*

Wehia had been a restless student, often too eager to start sparring before she had even mastered basic drills. She was surprised that her sword mistress hadn't given up on her. *"Use your head for once,"* her teacher had once snapped when Wehia had fumbled through one of the most basic drills and gotten her footwork all wrong. "You're not a sword master overnight, for Goddess's sake!"

Hadana t'Tolani was still waiting for her, the older swordswoman's legs planted wide on the ground, her sword pointed down. Her stance indicated that she was relaxed and ready to fight. By now, a crowd of forge women had gathered to watch the spectacle. Wehia ignored the glares and jeers, padding up to her aunt. She paused, straightening her back. Breathing through her nose, Wehia lifted Cold Steel up, hilt before her.

"Salutations," she said.

Hadana nodded, responding the same. "You have been taught well." She glanced at Cold Steel. "Yours?"

"My holding's heirloom," Wehia said, already watching out for weaknesses. Hadana leaned slightly on her left foot. An injury, perhaps, or a habit. "My great-grandmother's sword."

"Ah, the grand lady Shani t'Neela." Hadana's tone softened. "May her soul rest in peace."

Wehia hesitated. She had found Cold Steel in the

holding's armory, where they kept all the old swords and weapons. They might have been a small, knife-making holding, but in generations past, they had made swords, and they'd collected swords. She had walked in the armory, the dust motes, lit by her torch's light, swirling like fireflies. The rows and rows of swords, all scabbarded, looked as if they'd been sleeping, waiting for the day they would wake in the hands of new wielders.

Cold Steel had rested in a corner, set apart from the rest, longer than the other longswords. Wehia could tell that the sword had been exquisitely crafted. It had such a simplicity and perfection of form and line. Lifting it out from its cabinet, she'd felt an immediate connection, like tinder catching fire. The sword had called out to her and Wehia had known that it had to be with her. The blade was nicked and notched along its edges. It had been in fights before. She'd been stunned to find out—after much probing and questioning—that it had belonged to her great-grandmother. When she'd named it, it had been an affirmation. It had felt right, holding Cold Steel. Her great-grandmother would have been so proud of her. She'd asked her mother later why they had stopped making swords and her mother had become stonily silent. She was hiding something. What had happened?

Wehia's hesitation was all Hadana t'Tolani needed. She attacked.

The sword came down in a whistling arc, but Wehia

recovered her wits enough to block the strike with Cold Steel. She let the blow's energy flow down her arm and to the ground, earthed it, and backed away from Hadana, who was advancing cockily. Thus, the dance began, the duelists sizing each other up.

"Why don't you attack me?" Hadana challenged and the watching forge women laughed, hooting their encouragement to their champion.

Wehia kept silent because some swordswomen liked to heckle, as if words were weapons to whittle their opponents down to slivers of nothing. Wehia kept silent because she watched Hadana like a hunting fen-falcon. *"Watch for kinks in the armor,"* her sword mistress had instructed. What was Hadana afraid of? What was her main weakness?

Hadana came at her again, and Wehia blocked her. The swords cried out, the edges scraping with the screech of metal scratching metal. She recovered to deliver a side-strike, only to have Hadana evade it deftly. So, Hadana was an accomplished swordswoman.

Wehia found it odd that no daughter came forward to defend Hadana's honor, as daughters would stand beside their mother in times of challenge and duress. Sons were sent away to foster holdings. An idea grew in Wehia's mind and she smiled to herself.

"Ware!" Geri's voice shook Wehia out of her smugness, in time to see Hadana's sword an inch away from her nose. Wehia ducked and rolled out of Hadana's line of vision, cursing softly at her own carelessness.

"My niece vouches for you," Hadana said, laughing. The forge women echoed her, like cawing Baretti parrots, loudly derisive. Wehia caught sight of Geri's brassy hair and her nod and began to dance away from Hadana.

"No daughter to vouch for you?" Wehia challenged. The forge women fell silent and the forge became still. Swordsmithing only allowed women and girls, as the Sword Goddess had made it so. Their attention to detail and their endurance were what made swordsmithing such a privileged and exclusive skill and occupation. Men and boys were forbidden, as they were deemed too impatient and wanted speed over quality. Nieces and daughters of the holdings had a higher ranking and would stand beside the forge mistress to protect the forge in times of crisis or challenge.

Hadana's face darkened. She seemed to flinch at Wehia's words. "I am my own woman," Hadana snarled, baring her white teeth. Wehia had hit the right spot. Without fear, Wehia began to press her attack. The swords sang as they blocked cuts, delivered blows, and protected their wielders from harm.

Hadana t'Tolani was a good duelist, but she seemed to lean more to the right. Was there something wrong with her left foot? Was it an old injury or simply a personal quirk? Either way, it was an opening.

Wehia seized it.

Shouting the name of her family, Wehia pushed Hadana away, the cross guards of the swords screeching against one another. She kicked out with her foot, hitting Hadana's left shin. Hadana gasped and pulled away. Her eyes were wide, tendrils of her hair pressed flat on her skin. For a moment, her own sword wavered. Wehia swung Cold Steel down, the sharp tip at Hadana's throat.

The forge exploded in a tremendous sound-storm of song. The air filled with the noise of women wailing. For a moment, Wehia t'Doniyat was afraid that the forge women would sweep her up and attack her. Their fury was so great to behold. Then Hadana began to laugh once more, a throaty, robust laugh that went up to the roof of the forge and bounced off the walls like a gleeful winter spirit. The forge mistress sounded as if she had enjoyed the duel. She was not even offended.

"You have fighting spirit, daughter of swordsmith holding t'Doniyat." Hadana sheathed her sword and drew her forearm across her brow. "Your mother, my dear cousin, was right, after all. You do have a heart of steel."

"Was this just a test?" Wehia demanded, her entire being flushed with hot indignation, and the inexplicable feeling of . . . hope.

"Why not, niece? I am not going to admit just any apprentice into my holding without knowing what she's made of, more so for daughters from swordsmith holdings. Besides, I like a good duel . . . There's nothing like it to get the blood going."

The ululation grew louder. The song from the women was festive. Wehia, Cold Steel held against her like a talisman against the evil wilds, looked around her wearily, and warily too, unsure if she had won a victory or, indeed, the approval of the forge. Then she saw Geri among the forge women, and her smile gave Wehia courage.

CHAPTER 5

By the time Wehia Jirin t'Doniyat *ef* t'Tolani started her apprenticeship under Hadana t'Tolani, it was close to the Month of the Sword. Her name bore the new suffix for an apprentice not from the mistress's holding, marking her as part of the household. The t'Tolani and t'Doniyat were linked by blood line, but even then, tradition dictated the re-naming of an apprentice. Cousins and nieces were given the suffix *ef*, to denote their kinship connection to the holding. It simply meant "part of the holding." She had become part of the family.

Frost had crusted the main path leading to the forge, a layer of ice that cracked under fur-lined boots. The wind bite was the worst, piercing through the wool and right into bone. Everybody was grateful for the piping-hot stews and steamed waxed meat from the kitchen. During the nights, the women stoked the coals for the heaters. The generators pumped more energy. At least the holding was warm and sleep was comfortable. Wool and down blankets were provided. As cold as the season was, Wehia enjoyed it. It reminded her of the fens in winter.

In the freezing cold of the mornings, Wehia would look out of her bedroom window and see members from the ancient blood families in dawn processions. Most of them were on their way to the Council Hall or the Shrine, even in the frightful chill. The council sessions were conducted during the colder months so that they could plan for the coming year.

Haughty, clothed in finery, the men in embroidered fur coats, the women in elaborate gowns lined with wool, they paraded down the streets, bearing their staffs and scepters of power and escorted by liveried riders on horses. The horses too were gaily decorated, tassels and bells hanging from their bridles, their manes braided with colorful ribbons, their coats brushed to a high shine. Their breaths plumed white as they snorted and shook their heads.

Wrapped in furs, the footmen proudly carried banners embossed with the emblems of the blood families: a river hawk; a white lion from the snowy mountain ridges; a marsh kingfisher; a fen stag; sea serpents coiling above waves—Wehia was sure she hadn't seen all the blood family emblems yet. The heraldry was dazzling. People would stop to watch the processions, seeming not to mind the cold!

Metakse had no ruling family, no monarch. Not

anymore. Once, there had been an unjust ruler who had been overthrown by the blood families, the most powerful families in the land, each one controlling a particular ministry, trade, or industry. Titles lingered but were no more than reminders of a more tumultuous past.

The Council comprised representatives of the blood families. Decisions were made by vote. No one family was meant to wield more power than another, but everyone knew that, in reality, the key members of the Council, the ones whose words held the most sway, were from the wealthier families.

Wehia knew that the main blood families lived in spired and towered palaces, while those from less important houses inhabited more modest, but still grand mansions. The palaces and mansions rose around the basilica, as if to protect it, their soaring spires and towers like rows of forbidding spears and blades. The swordsmith holdings and other buildings sprawled outwards like layers of fortification. The blood living in the fen—the fen families—dwelled in fine manses surrounded by shrubland. They were often the cadet branches of City clans. Some governed minor portions of the land.

⊢———

The forge now served as a classroom where Hadana stood not just as forge mistress, but also teacher. The first few lessons were on sword makes, types of steel used for these sword makes, and the lineages behind each significant sword made by the mistresses of lore. Hadana explained the different sword blades and their marks. She took a book from the holding's library and opened it before Wehia's rapt eyes. It was a simple book with a cover of blue, the holding's color. The inside pages were what mattered: an archive of all the holdings' sword marks (symbols, patterns or other signs unique to registered sword makers, which confirmed the authenticity of a weapon), from the smallest of holdings situated close to the borders of the fen lands to the large and prosperous ones in the City of Swords.

Her mother had shown her a version of this, except that the t'Tolani's book contained more, including the bloodlines that were the originators of the marks. The script was neat and tight, written in ink of a strong, glossy blackness—most likely Verusian black!

Hadana carefully turned the pages until she found the one she had in mind. The familiar crest of the t'Tolani: the swooping crane with spread wings. The mark was outlined in silver—it glinted in the light of the forge's study room. *Jessian* silver? Wehia gasped—Jessian silver and Verusian black inks, both fine and expensive.

Hadana proceeded to turn the pages, again with gentle hands. Wehia saw the t'Doniyat mark of a canine's head, outlined too, with black ink. But this one bore sharp teeth and was edged in an ochre-red ink. Mother hadn't told her about this variant mark.

"You come from proud stock, Wehia Jirin t'Doniyat—a family who has made more than just kitchen knives," Hadana said, closing the book reverently with gnarled yet gentle hands and placing it back on the shelf. More than just kitchen knives . . . Yes, a long time ago, they had made longswords of breathtaking quality. The swords in her holding's armory had been made by them; Cold Steel one of them! But her mother wouldn't even speak of their history. Again, the doubt returned. Was her mother hiding something? What had they done to end up knife-makers instead?

"We share a common ancestress: Yin t'Idan. In your blood runs her blood. You will make swords to be wielded by powerful people. You will make *legends*.

"But for now, young woman, you need to learn the basics of sword-making all over again. To be sure, one does not learn to make a sword in just a year or two. Your mother knows that. You need a longer length of study and practice, Wehia. I propose you complete your senior apprenticeship with me so that you can have a better grounding in blade making. And, eventually, I hope you will achieve your forge woman status."

"You do not learn to make a sword in a year or two." Would she have to wait that long? Wehia bit her lip. Oh, she knew that she was *supposed* to wait, that it would be some time before she was deemed ready, but . . . she *felt* ready! Was it foolish of her to think she could do it? How her mother would laugh, but Wehia felt ready.

Hadana was tracing the spines of the books on the shelf with a faraway expression.

"A sword is not just a piece of steel," said the forge mistress. "It will come to life when you fold your will into its making. Your breath infuses its creation. It is a live thing, if you don't know it already. It has its own will. Know the basics because a lost step will cost many. A mistake, even a minor one, will warp the sword forever."

As much as she hated having to learn the basics again, Wehia was determined to listen to Hadana: She wanted to make her sword!

"Child, imagine you are making a baby . . ." Hadana's lips twitched. "Sit down. Stop frowning. It's only an analogy. *If* you are making a baby, you will need to have a good environment—you will need to have a healthy body; you will need to eat well, rest well."

Wehia Jirin t'Doniyat ef t'Tolani had never intended to get married to some boy and have babies. The idea had never pleased her. However, the baby-making analogy made sense.

"What happens if the maker is unhealthy?" Wehia asked. The sounds of the busy forge were muffled through the walls of the study. Work was still work, even during winter, but now, Wehia's attention rested solely on her aunt. Aunt Hadana's handsome face bore a sad expression. Wehia had never seen Hadana looking so grey and distraught.

"Then you pay with your life," she said, and her voice was bleak.

When Wehia was done with the lessons, it was back to the forge, where she had to shadow Hadana constantly. Her aunt wanted her there for every single step of sword-making, every single idea, from the design of a fenlady's protective talisman to the melting of various alloys and metals in crucibles.

"Make the right decisions," Hadana said behind her mask as forge women in similar protective wear poured molten tin and copper into a cylindrical crucible. "The right mix of metals is important. You have to be precise with the composition."

"Hold this ladle for me. Watch how you hold it! There is an art to holding the ladle."

So the teaching continued while the Month of the Knife brought in the snow flurries and, on some nights, snowstorms. The forge women bundled up in furs and continued working in the forge. The signal fires on the roofs of all the holdings still burned brightly, watched by keen-eyed guardian women appointed for this important task.

Some nights saw the forge women—aunts, daughters, cousins, and daughters-in-law—gather around the hearth-fire in the center of the dining hall, such a large, echoing place with soaring rafters and solid concrete walls. They sang their holding's songs, their hands beating familiar and unfamiliar rhythms on their frame drums. The songs spoke of the promise of spring, of the shovels that turned the soil and planted the seeds, of the hammers that repaired the roofs and walls ruined by the cold, and the promise of work from the various lands, bringing more wealth and prestige to the holding.

Wehia would sit in a corner, her arms around her chest, feeling the sharp kiss of homesickness. She knew that, at her own holding, her aunts and cousins would have been doing the same thing, singing around the hearth. Their frame drums were smaller. They called them "dommet drums." The sound was lighter but no less soulful. The t'Tolani's drums were deeper, like the rumble of some storm-tossed sea or sky; the music tugged at Wehia's heart and palpitated her insides like the hunt-growls of large felines from the fens and mountain ridges. She wished suddenly for open spaces, for shrublands and trees. She missed the sharp fragrances of resin and sap. She would sleep and dream of running along the bog, with the ore dogs, silver swirls curling up the gnarly-trunked trees.

Geri often sat beside her during the drumming. Geri encouraged her to join in with the rest of the singers and, sometimes, Wehia sang the songs, those with lyrics similar to the ones the t'Doniyat sang. Geri was so friendly, warm and kind. Was she also lonely, like Wehia? After all, most of the women, including the other senior apprentices, were older than they were and kept to themselves. Wehia did not object to being befriended. She liked Geri, who had a certain strength beneath her gentleness, like steel beneath soft velvet—beautiful Geri did the same backbreaking, tedious apprentice jobs, but unlike others, she didn't complain. Besides, companionship was companionship, no matter its shape.

During the bitter winter nights, Geri's presence was a much appreciated down blanket. Wehia often looked forward to seeing Geri after a long day at the forge. Geri made her smile and feel warm inside. She had also begun to feel a certain tenderness towards Geri. She wanted to protect Geri, who was such a beautiful person, inside and out. Wehia wondered . . . Geri was so attentive towards her . . . was she trying to tell Wehia something?

Wehia didn't know what to think. Growing up in the t'Doniyat holding, she had had no shortage of nieces and cousins to play with. However, she was not used to having friends. She was deemed too outspoken and often said the wrong things at the wrong time. She didn't like making small talk, either. Her nieces and cousins had kept to their own age and peer groups. Even in a household filled with kinswomen, Wehia had often been alone. She'd loved wandering the fens by herself, the sky, the trees, and the ore dogs her only companions. She'd hardly met other apprentices outside the holding.

Geri was her first real friend, someone whom she could talk to without fear of rejection. She was not surprised at the rush of tenderness she felt in her heart for the girl. She liked Geri and she wanted the friendship to continue further, even after her apprenticeship. She would miss Geri. The fierceness of this thought made her heart pound. Did Geri feel the same way? She prayed to the Goddess that Geri felt the same.

But of late, Geri seemed distracted. She often

appeared anxious, wringing her hands. When Wehia asked what was wrong, Geri said that there were some challenging commissions they had to complete before the next month started, and all the experienced apprentices were given more tasks and responsibilities. Wehia didn't question Geri further. She had seen how industrious and attentive Geri was at the forge.

In truth, Geri should have been done with her apprenticeship. She had far more experience than Wehia and was so capable; but the young woman had once mentioned that she was not yet ready to be a forge woman. Curious, Wehia had later asked why she desired such a long apprenticeship—much longer than the already lengthy learning period.

"I feel . . . that I can't move on just yet," Geri had explained patiently. "Hadana feels the same way. After my mother's passing, I wanted . . . more time . . . to heal, to be whole again. My heart didn't feel it was time for me to end my apprenticeship. It still doesn't feel ready. I hope you understand . . ."

"I do, I do!" Wehia replied quickly, her face burning. She felt bad for making Geri speak of something so personal, and for bringing up the sad matter of her mother's passing.

The t'Tolani holding was wrapped up in a flurry of activity. The house servants decorated the main hall with strings of firecrackers and the kitchen staff made sausages. Laughter filled the holding as forge women gossiped about attending the weddings and pair-bonding ceremonies of their friends. There was a festive feel in the air. Wehia helped the kitchen women. All apprentices were busy with their assigned tasks.

Geri, who was also helping in the kitchen, was unusually quiet, the silence thick about her like a shroud. Wehia felt as if the sun were hiding behind clouds. While they worked, they listened to the kitchen staff talk about marriages and all the juicy morsels about various lords and ladies. They were also generous with their needle when it came to forge women from other holdings. Wehia noticed Geri shrinking into herself as the jokes became louder and bawdier. She had never seen Geri so affected before.

"Are you feeling unwell?" Wehia whispered cautiously. The kitchen itself was redolent with the odors of animal intestines, minced meat, spices, and sausages being boiled in huge, copper cauldrons. Back home, she would often try to flee the holding when they made sausages. The smell of blood and offal was nauseating. They often had to mask the odor by mixing in spices and herbs. Even then, the smell was intense. No wonder some of the kitchen women had to duck out for some fresh air!

Geri shook her head. "I am well," she said, but her expression indicated otherwise. She went back to scouring the already gleaming pots with a vengeance.

"What is wrong, Geri? I have never seen you this unhappy before." Wehia pushed on despite being afraid she might say the wrong thing. Was Geri unhappy? Geri's face looked glum, as if she did not want to stay any longer in the kitchen. That was unlike Geri, who usually tackled every task with good cheer.

"They laugh at women who are in loveless marriages and mock them for their choices," Geri said softly. "How do we know what is behind their decisions? They should be pitied, not made fun of."

"Is that what's bothering you?" Wehia asked. "Their talk? Should I ask them to stop? They should stop if their gossip upsets you."

"No, no, no!" Geri waved her hands anxiously. She smiled weakly. "I am well. Don't worry about me."

"But it seems you are still unhappy. I don't like to see you unhappy. You have been unhappy lately."

Geri sighed, throwing the sponge she held into the soapy water. It splashed hard, spraying white suds all over. "I have many things on my mind. That's all."

"You can talk to me. I am your friend."

Geri's warm smile returned. "Thank you, Wehia. I know you are. I am just . . . just saddened by the fact that people go into marriages without love or even trust. That there are men who think they are the Goddess's gift to everyone. What a world we live in!"

"I agree that there should be love and trust in a marriage. I think forced marriages are not permitted . . ."

"They are not," Geri said with an edge in her voice. She reached out to touch Wehia's hand gently before scooping up the sponge up again. She then lapsed into silence once more, leaving Wehia feeling befuddled and worried.

The lighting of firecrackers signaled the end of the Month of the Knife. The City rang with the *rat-tat-tat* of a multitude of firecrackers exploding at once. The white roofs and iced streets suddenly glowed a warm amber as the firecrackers and fireworks turned the City festive once more. The brief celebration heralded the hardest month of all: the Saber, named thus because this was the season when brigands were the most prosperous, especially in the low fen areas where patrols were few. The Month of the Saber was also the last month for the skinning of the remaining fattened livestock. The hides were turned into clothing or footwear or used for musical instruments; the meat was made into sausages and plant fertilizer.

The t'Tolani forge had a firecracker ceremony and more singing with the drums. They let off the long strings of red-papered firecrackers and there was a lot of shouting and loud laughter as the firecrackers burst and exploded. The fireworks holdings made these tubes of gunpowder. They were as proud as the swordsmith holdings of their particular craft and guarded their secrets just as fiercely as the forges.

For the firecracker ceremony, Wehia was given a bowl of sliced blood sausages and a hardboiled egg the size of a newborn's fist.

After the ceremony, Geri drew Wehia to the courtyard, where it was peaceful. They walked along the courtyard, listening to the other firecracker ceremonies happening in the City. Everybody was celebrating. It was at once boisterous and chaotic. Wehia was just happy she could stay in the middle of a quiet courtyard and enjoy the company of a very good friend.

Hadana t'Tolani showed Wehia a book of sword designs. This book had another simple, nondescript blue cover.

"Longswords," the forge mistress said. "Look at the designs carefully. Analyze them. Understand them. Know them. They speak a language you need to be able to comprehend before you make one."

So, for the Month of the Saber, Wehia pored over the book, jotting down thoughts and observations as she studied each longsword design. They each did speak a different language. One type had tapered sharp edges, almost like praying hands. Another type was slim, delicate at first glance, although looks could be deceiving, for it was known to cut deep. This type of longsword was well loved by the fen lords and ladies as a dueling sword. It sang to Wehia immediately, however, like a harp string pulled by a skillful finger, reminding her of Cold Steel; it was effectively Cold Steel's relative. Her kin. Wehia traced the true lines of the longsword design, her eyes closing. She could hear its song. A distinct song, not one with words—swords never spoke in words—but with a distinct tune, softly hummed. Her entire being vibrated, resonating with the song.

"The Faith sword line and type," Wehia whispered to herself, making the name a part of herself. This was the bloodline of Cold Steel, like the bloodline that ran through the t'Tolani and t'Doniyat, and all the many swordsmith families. She liked how the name flowed, like silver curves and swirls but edged in deep blue. So it had links with the t'Tolani and their cadet branches. But it was also linked to her, to her family, because the t'Doniyat shared the same ancestress. "The Faith line: belief true and true." The sword was part of her heritage.

Bathed in the golden glow of the study lamp, Wehia was suddenly homesick once more, longing for the ore-rich bogs and the loyal canines who followed her family's forge women everywhere. She missed Saki and Toma, her favorite ore dogs. She missed the trees and the blue skies. She once more felt so out of place with the t'Tolani, whose appearance was similar to hers and yet so different. She missed her holding's study room, where she spent hours poring over books. Here, the room lacked the warmth of her home. Kin, yet so different. The t'Doniyat were fen people, more familiar with shrubs and open spaces. The t'Tolani were city folk, comfortable with buildings and complex streets. The difference made Wehia feel sad.

She sighed and went back to her studies. There were a few more designs to look at, to understand, and to love. Yet she knew, deep inside, that she had already decided. The decision might have been premature, but it was as solid as ore and as firm as untempered steel, just as had been her decision to apprentice herself under Mistress Hadana t'Tolani. She must remain unwavering.

"Stop waffling," Mother had often scolded her when she'd seemed distracted at the forge. *"You cannot be a good smith if you have a mind that wanders the fens all the time."* And she did wander the fens, exploring the bog and running

with the ore-dogs. The open sky, the fresh air, and the stars that shone uncovered by clouds. She often felt cooped up in the holding. The first impulse for her when her chores were done had beento wander through the trees of the fen with the ore dogs beside her.

Wehia's fingers traced the shape of the Faith sword pattern, listening to its contours, to the music they made. How could she be mistaken when she heard the sword's song so clearly? It was time to make manifest her dream.

Wehia reached for the ink pot and opened herself to the song.

CHAPTER 6

"I AM SO TIRED," said Wehia to Geri when they met to eat their midday meal one day. They shared freshly baked buns. Wehia broke hers apart, delighting in the delicious aroma of minced meat and spices. She was ravenously hungry.

"Apprenticeship is tiring," Geri said wryly, blowing on her bun to cool it.

"They are making me do everything. *Everything*. I have done it all, at home. I thought I could move ahead . . ." Wehia grimaced as she rubbed her arm muscles. They were sore. Her fingers ached.

Geri looked at her closely. Her eyes were kind. "You sound frustrated. I can understand why. But . . . isn't this the same at your holding? Surely, you have done the same tasks in your home forge."

"But that's it. I have done it all, over and over, at my mother's holding, but now it's as if I am a beginner."

"Just because you have some grounding doesn't mean you know everything," said Geri softly.

Annoyed, Wehia chewed her bun, knowing that Geri was right. Why was she still complaining? She should have been familiar with the rigors of the forge, shouldn't she've?

"My aunt wants you to have a solid foundation," Geri said, licking her fingers clean. "She expects the same from all her forge women and apprentices. She does not like rushing into things. Making a sword . . . any blade . . . is a major undertaking."

"I know," Wehia whispered.

Geri gave Wehia's arm a gentle squeeze. "You can do it. I believe in you."

The afternoon meal was soon over. Pairs and small groups of women left the dining hall.

Wehia returned reluctantly to the forge, where more tasks awaited. She promised herself to work hard. She had come all the way to the City to make a sword—her sword—hadn't she?

For the next two months, Wehia carried out all the tasks required of her dutifully. She assisted the forge women in all tasks, no matter how seemingly menial, forcing herself to focus on the work and not be distracted by the niggling impatience that was always gnawing away in her heart of hearts. It was not so bad. The forge women told her stories and shared tips they had picked up after years of forge work. Wehia came to cherish these moments, enjoying the camaraderie and the feeling of being accepted and included. If only Hadana would show her approval more clearly, though. Wehia could never quite tell what the forge mistress thought of her work and progress. The most she got from Hadana was a nod. Somehow, that nod and her aunt's grim expression made Wehia intensely annoyed. Still, she clenched her teeth and persevered.

Back in her room, each evening, Wehia would enjoy a hot soak in her tub and then go straight to bed, sinking into a deep slumber seconds after her head touched her pillow. The next morning, she would wake, refreshed, eager to begin a new day and continue her training, hopeful that Hadana would give her a sign that all was well.

In all honesty, Wehia willed the days to pass quickly so that she would arrive more quickly at the moment when she could begin to make her sword. When would that moment come? Hadana seemed adamant that Wehia should repeat, endlessly, every step of the sword-making process. Mornings were spent studying sword-making books, while Wehia worked under the supervision of the forge women, or Hadana herself, in the afternoons.

"You should not see it as a chore," Hadana said as she inspected one of Wehia's half-worked blades. "It should already be part of your life, as familiar as breathing. Now, look at this blade. The edges have a few nicks. Your filing is uneven. Were you paying attention? Did your mind wander off again?"

Wehia nodded mutely and went back to filing the blade, forcing herself to concentrate. The apprentices at her holding went through a similar process, which took years, before they became full-fledged forge women.

Four months passed swiftly by. Wehia began to feel like a part of the t'Tolani forge. Every waking moment was spent in it. She slept, breathed, and ate *forge*.

Besides all the tasks, she ran errands for the forge women. She enjoyed the brief forays out of the forge, relishing the sights and sounds of the City. The aromas of street food, the sweet burnt candy smell of toffee and roast nuts, made her mouth water. With her apprentice allowance of dagger-coins, Wehia sampled some of the delicious food, especially relishing the crunchy, sweet texture of toffee fruit. They were affordable—two or three dagger-coins—and she enjoyed eating them as treats.

She thrilled at the chiming of the bells from the Shrine. The City dazzled her, although some sights still bewildered her, especially the beggars who slept along the roadsides and stern soldiers sitting on their huge horses guarding the various intersections. However, Wehia didn't let these experiences faze her. She loved the City. It was so different from the quiet fens where she'd been born. Everything felt more colorful and exciting.

Her struggles during these arduous months made her miss her mother and her holding more than ever. She must not disappoint Rohana. She must return triumphant, with her sword, the sword she'd promised she would make.

But, as Geri constantly reminded her, Hadana would not be easily persuaded to let her begin working on her own blade.

"It's not just about being able to make a whole sword, or dagger," said Geri. "She makes you do everything again and again to train your patience. Being patient is the most important skill a sword maker can possess. I am sure you have heard my aunt say so."

Wehia made a sour face, and Geri laughed.

"The forge work is not the worst of it," said Wehia. "The books are the worst. So many. Too many."

"I remember. I too had to read all the books. I still have to. There are many—I don't think we will ever be done with them!" Geri laughed.

"Not more books!" Wehia groaned.

"Theoretical knowledge reinforces the actual swordmaking," said Geri.

Wehia heaved a loud sigh. She had also heard that phrase from Hadana.

"Do you think you are ready to make your sword?" Geri asked.

"I . . . don't know. I feel I am ready. But . . ." Wehia shook her head.

"My aunt doesn't think so?" Geri's voice was kind.

Wehia shrugged. "I have not mentioned it. It never seems to be the right time. She never seems happy with me."

"She wants the best. She's never happy with apprentices who are simply good. You must be excellent, beyond her expectations. Apprenticeship is hard. For many, it feels like it's never-ending. Be patient. You will get there."

A few days later, Hadana told Wehia to read about scabbard and pommel types: round, hexagonal, half-moon, nut-shaped, perfume-stopper—the pommel types were myriad and bewildering, arranged accordingly to specific time periods and styles. Hadn't she read about this all before, at her own holding? She recalled hours of reading, as well as helping her mother and aunts in the holding's workshop. She also recalled being immensely distracted and bored. It felt like watching paint dry.

Together with the other junior apprentices, Wehia was tasked with carving scabbards and shaping hilts and pommels. Each eight-day was spent making the different components of these parts, over and over again. As an apprentice, Wehia had to be familiar with the types of metal and wood used in this work. Sometimes, there was even a merging of both, for more complex sword designs. The wood most favored was aromatic heartwood with a rich, distinctive, dark-red center, almost like blood. The metal was styled and crafted from the forge itself. Wehia sawed, cut, carved, and filed wood. She hammered, shaped, and folded, finding some solace beating pommels into shape. At least the reading was done with! The time she spent with the other apprentices was pleasant. They exchanged small talk, jokes, and anecdotes. Wehia excelled at making scabbards, finally earning some warm praise from Hadana and the senior forge women.

Wehia also helped in the design of scabbards, learning how to make measurements with ruler and charcoal on thin drafting paper. She loved writing the numbers on the crinkly, blue paper. She admired her work, earning exasperated looks from the forge women. They laughed uproariously and rolled their eyes.

"Be careful when you measure the length and width,"

said Hadana, shaking her head. Her face bore a frown that seemed permanent to Wehia. "So that it will fit the blade once it is done."

For the hilts, Wehia used strips of fine, black leather or thin, silver wire. Some swords had ornate basket hilts crafted to protect the wielder's hand. They were hard to make, requiring the forge woman to be highly skilled as a smith and artisan, weaving stripes of steel into handles that resembled baskets curving inward like river shells. These swords were considered exquisite and uncommon. As usual, Hadana and the senior forge women supervised the apprentices, inspecting their work and providing guidance for those who needed more time.

Eventually, on her tenth month of apprenticeship with the t'Tolani holding, Wehia learned how to join all the various parts: blade, cross guard, hilt, and pommel. Again, under the watchful eye of Hadana and the forge women, she welded the blade and guard. She slipped the hilt over the tang so that it rested on the blade shoulder of the sword. The pommel was screwed onto the tang. She wanted to make sure that the parts wouldn't come loose.

When everything was done, the sword was given a final buffing and polishing. Wehia worked it over a whetstone to sharpen the edges further.

Hadana examined the finished product critically. To Wehia, the sword was beautiful. Like Cold Steel. Perfect, right from sharp tip to shining, hexagonal pommel. She found no fault in it.

"Making a sword is not just the creation of its blade, scabbard, and pommel," the forge mistress said quietly, placing the sword down on the worktable. Everyone turned to watch her speak. "It takes many months, years, to perfect your craft."

Wehia readied herself for a reprimand. Where had she gone wrong? She had done everything the t'Tolani forge mistress expected and demanded. She had been meticulous, hadn't she?

She said, "I know," earning a sharp glance from Hadana.

"You did the tasks well, Wehia," the forge mistress finally said. "So did the rest of the apprentices."

CHAPTER 7

The autumn months of the Flint, Hook, and Sword passed swiftly. This was traditionally a very busy time when the year's calves were weaned and starchy tubers harvested at the farms and plantations. At the end of autumn, as the weather got colder, livestock was brought in from pasture; the male calves were castrated and rams sold.

These months made Wehia wistful. Back at her holding, the women would have been selling off their year's batch of knives at the market. Wehia missed the laughter and the songs sung by the women at their family forge. She quashed her homesickness by keeping busy. She also spent more time with Geri during meals. She enjoyed these moments. They made the three months more bearable.

By the end of the Flint, the kitchen women finished making the last batch of sausages and the holding celebrated with a small feast. The sausages were grilled and lavishly drizzled with a sweet sauce. However, ever prudent and resourceful, the kitchen women kept some of the sausages to last the holding through winter along with the waxed meats. The holding's apprentices helped them stock the larder and cellar. It would be the same throughout the City and the fens.

During the months of the Knife and Saber, Wehia continued working and learning at the forge. It was now too cold to go out into the open. People stayed indoors. Everything came to a standstill. Even trade and commerce slowed down. Only a few daring street vendors stood at street corners to sell piping-hot honeyed fried fritters and mulled spiced wine to those who ventured out for quick errands.

At the forge, the t'Tolani forgewomen worked on last-minute commissions and checked the holding's stores. The winter months were also stocktaking months when they assessed their inventory. The apprentices assisted them while they combed through their stocks methodically, noting what they needed for the new year, especially for the Month of the Plow when planning for the year began. That month was when farmers began breaking the earth to get it ready for the sowing of seeds.

Determined to stay focused, Wehia juggled the time between helping out with the rest of the apprentices and finding time to work on her sword design. Geri believed in her. Wehia drew strength from that.

I can do this, she told herself. *I can do this.*

When she had time to herself, Wehia liked walking in the courtyard. Deep in winter, it was bare. No jewel colors darted about, for the Stolati hummers were hibernating in their tiny nests. Beyond the courtyard's stone walls, the City moved sluggishly, like a river heavy with ice and solemn with the cold. The shrubs and trees in the fens would be covered with frost. How was her holding doing? Did they have enough to eat? Were the heaters working? Had her mother put out cushions for the ore dogs? How quickly time had passed!

Wehia met Geri in the courtyard. Geri was wrapped in the thickest of shawls and wools. Her brassy hair peeked out of the vibrant-blue headcover. Her eyes, the brightest of amber, shone. Wehia liked those eyes. They reminded her of the sunlight shimmering through the leaves of trees. For a while, they circled the courtyard in silence. Wehia glanced at Geri, who seemed to be deep in thought, gazing into the distance. She was lovely to look at. Wehia felt a pang in her heart, a rush of sharp tenderness. Her mind then turned to her studies, her sword, and her holding.

"The lunch bell just rang," Geri said, breaking Wehia's reverie. "There is morani stew today, with rye bread and mashed dried pulses."

Wehia's stomach rumbled at the mention of morani stew. It was one of the kitchen's specialties, a favorite winter warmer. Her holding had their own version.

They continued to walk around the courtyard as forge women, chatting animatedly in pairs and in groups, filtered into the dining hall.

"Do you still feel as if you are a stranger here?" Geri asked. The question was abrupt. The expression in the eyes gazing at her was, thankfully, not accusatory. They held only a gentle curiosity.

Wehia felt the sudden hot sting of tears and the rush of bile in her throat. She could only nod.

"It won't always be so, I promise," Geri said reassuringly. "Just wait . . . Once they get to know you better, it will be different. How about my aunt? Is she still cold towards you?"

"Not so much, but I think she's the distant type," said Wehia. "She's not the teacher I expected."

"My aunt is a hard woman, but she is also kind," Geri said, placing a soft hand on Wehia's arm. The touch jolted Wehia, like spring lightning flickering on the holding's moors. "She sees you as a daughter of our line, which is a good thing. Her sons are not like that. By the sword's curve, my cousins hardly see their blood mother at all."

"Hadana t'Tolani bore only sons?" Wehia asked. "No daughters?"

"Only sons. No daughters. Some of the girls you see

are fostered from other blood-related holdings. Some are adopted into the family by Hadana and her cousins so that they are given places at the forge. To us, they are considered our blood kin."

Wehia had seen similar cases in her own holding where girls had been brought in from other holdings. Nieces. Cousins. By apprenticing under Hadana, Wehia herself was considered a member of the t'Tolani line. Sons, nephews, and male cousins, however, were treated differently.

"Our nephews and male cousins are sent away to work at the farms and plantations," Geri said. "Your holding practices the same tradition, I think?"

"Yes."

Wehia had seen some of the forge women in her holding carrying baby boys and toddlers. Those were her cousins. They were lovingly treated and cared for by her aunts, but once they reached the age of eight, they were sent away to work and fostered in other places like the farms and orchards owned by the holding. It was the way of swordsmiths. She had male cousins who'd spent only a short time at the holding before they'd left. During some festivals, they were permitted to visit so that they could celebrate with the rest of the holding, but the swordsmith holdings were essentially matrilineal: Skills passed from mother to daughter.

"Be it sons or daughters, some of us will end up

marrying within the holdings so that the line remains strong," Geri said. "Some will end up marrying someone not of the holding. I confess I don't know everything about marriage. It's confusing." She smiled weakly and looked sad.

Wehia frowned. She knew that marital unions between members of swordsmith holdings were common. These unions were to strengthen the ties between the holdings. There were also occasional alliances with blood families. A son of a blood family might ask for the hand of a daughter of a swordsmith holding. It had happened before, and with the express approval of both sides. Some holdings and blood families were related to each other to some degree, with alliances sealed and forged throughout the generations.

"My mother says we swordsmiths are practical." Wehia rolled her eyes at the memory. "I don't understand marriage, either."

Geri's expression brightened. The mood lifted.

Practical. That was the word. Many alliances were made not just by marriage, but also by trade. Men born of the holdings were free to seek their partners outside the clans. Forge women sought mates from trading houses and farms. Wehia's father was a plantation owner. She seldom saw him, though she knew her mother still maintained a cordial relationship with the man.

She could not imagine being married and having

children. She gazed at Geri and wondered if her friend had dreams of being a wife and mother. Somehow, she hoped not. Oh, that was selfish and unkind, but . . .

Wehia took a deep breath. "You have been kind to me, Geri," she said slowly. "I'm grateful for you, your care and kindness, your *presence*. I am grateful for your friendship."

"I am not your friend to be kind, Wehia."

"I-I am glad."

Geri smiled.

Wehia could not help herself. "Do . . . do you . . . *like* me, Geri?" she blurted out.

Geri turned away, presenting her profile, the upturned curve of her lips. Wehia's heart leaped—Geri's cheeks were flushed and the girl had started to tremble.

"Oh, Geri," whispered Wehia, her heart now soaring. "I see . . . I *see*."

"Please keep it a secret," Geri said, her voice small, like a trapped songbird. Wehia must have tender, caring hands. This bird wanted to flee out of sheer fear. The moment felt as fragile as lake ice. Or a blade newly forged, its steel in the in-between stage, half-formed.

"Please, Wehia, I liked you the moment I first saw you."

Wehia's heart fluttered. "Oh, Geri."

The two girls froze with fright when they heard laughter. It was only a group of senior forge women passing through the courtyard. They didn't pay attention to the two girls.

"I wanted to tell you . . . I like you. I-I wanted to tell you because . . . once you make your sword, you will be gone. You will go back to your holding. I might never see you again."

"Oh, Geri, please don't say that!"

Geri inhaled deeply. "It's out now, and I feel so much better. Do you . . . like me? We are linked by a common ancestress . . . but . . . do—do you . . . *will* you like me?"

"Oh, Geri . . . *of course* I like you!" said Wehia. Her shoulders suddenly felt lighter with this confession. Geri looked relieved too—her face brightened with joy and her eyes sparkled.

She leaned forward, her fingers curling around Geri's. Their gloves creaked. Wehia wanted to peel hers off and touch Geri's skin. Her emotions spun. She didn't know what to say, except a breathless *yes, yes, yes!* They needed no words to express this affirmation, this connection. She had never liked boys, anyway. She found them almost impossible to understand. Geri made her smile. Geri made her feel strong.

Their eyes met, amber to amber.

Their fingers laced together, tightening. Although the moment felt as delicate as spun sugar, Wehia had never felt stronger and happier in her life.

Then they pulled apart, as quickly as spun sugar

melts, because the lunch bell rang again, for stragglers to have their meals. Time waited for no woman. The forge worked on a tight timetable of hard work and never paused. Giggling, the two girls hurried to the kitchen, where they shared a bowl of morani stew and broke the hard-crusted rye bread together.

When Wehia returned to the heated study and back to the sword design currently half-drawn on the parchment paper, she wove the joy into it as well, singing to herself, singing to the *sword soon-to-be*.

CHAPTER 8

THE CITY OF SWORDS heaved a collective sigh of relief when the Month of the Plow reached its end. Its departure was marked by a vicious snowstorm that blanketed the roofs and streets in white and threatened to put out the signal fires. It was with diligence and sheer determination of their keepers that the fires did not go out, even in the howling wind and heavy sleet. When the snowstorm ceased and people dared peek from their holding doors and windows, warm plum cider was shared amongst family and close friends to mark the end of the snow as well as the month. Anticipation rose for the Month of the Shovel, when pilgrims and worshipers brought their shovels, white candles, and small bags of ore-chips as offerings to the Shrine. It was a month of thanksgiving too, the celebration of having survived the harsh winter months.

The forge grew busy once more. The entire building, from courtyard to rooms, was swept clean by all the women and girls of the holding. Windows were flung open wide to let the fresh air in. Down blankets and other bed linen were washed and aired; old mattresses were replaced; robes and gowns were soaked in suds and given a thorough rinsing. The holding's laundry rang with the sound of women working, some making sure the water ran continuously hot. Wehia marveled at the amount of wood and coal used to power the steam generators, which then provided the lighting and the heat for the holding.

The forge functioned smoothly because of steam. All blood families had steam, of course—the ability to own steam generators or engines indicated your level of wealth. Being able to generate that much steam showed that the t'Tolani was a wealthy swordsmith holding. And ambitious too. They not only profited from their fine commissions, but also owned farms, livestock, and orchards.

In lean times, according to Geri, they relied on the coastal holdings for fish and dried kelp. They also did trading along the River Verru, the great river weaving through the City. By now, the river had begun to thaw. Boats trawled for ice fish.

Wehia thought of her own humble holding. By now, it would have been carrying out its own spring cleaning. She remembered the chores she'd had to do—the mopping of floors and scrubbing of tiles that she had considered tedious, but that she now missed, painfully.

Her holding had always lived modestly. They depended on a small steam generator that formed the backbone of the forge and the heating. Like many holdings, they reared their own cattle for milk and kept a couple of cows in a shed, besides having a small farm. When the commissions slowed, the t'Doniyat made their own cheese and pastries that they sold in the fen markets. The fortunes of a forge ebbed and flowed, but Wehia's life had always been comfortable. Her bed was warm, food was always on the table, and work was often waiting for her in their little forge. Now, having seen more of the world, she had to admit that she had been spoiled and she was ashamed that she had had all these luxuries and privileges. Wehia had seen how the City was unforgiving to the poor, especially in the bitter cold of winter. As a t'Tolani apprentice, she had made a few trips out of the t'Tolani holding to run errands and chores for Hadana and personally witnessed the City's harshness.

Behind the marbled grandeur and the imposing statues, beggars huddled in corners of alleyways, faces gaunt, lean with want. Wehia had tried to dodge them— men, women, even children—when she'd gone on errands. The first time she had encountered a beggar, a woman with iron-grey hair, she'd been shocked by how frail the woman had looked. The blanket she'd worn around her thin shoulders had been threadbare, barely warm enough. The woman had tried to sell her trinkets, woven straw and hair. They'd lain on a rag, a few rusted coins resting beside them. Wehia remembered that everything had been shaped like a sun with five rays spreading out from its center.

"Please, buy my sunburst—I have to feed my children," said the old woman in querulous tones.

The cold was biting and all Wehia had wanted to do was deliver a box of tools to another holding, two streets away from the t'Tolani holding.

She hated walking through the narrow winding alleyways, and the woman had frightened her. With staring eyes, she had pressed one sunburst into Wehia's hand, and, gazing at the unfortunate creature, Wehia had suddenly realized that the woman was not as old as she had first thought. It was hardship and starvation that had aged her prematurely.

"I need to go," Wehia had muttered as she'd hurried away, dropping the sunburst. *"Sorry."* She didn't think the woman had heard her. The clatter of approaching horses had shattered the silence. The woman had fled from the scene. A regiment of blood family soldiers, clad in winter tunics and furs, had trotted down the alleyway.

The encounter had reminded Wehia uncomfortably of the border people who lived at the margins of society and were often seen begging for food in the fen markets. Many were dressed in similar rags to what the woman had worn and were often dependent on the generosity of strangers for food and coin. Wehia didn't know how to feel about the border people. She felt sorry for them, but was also irritated by the trouble and mess they caused. They often squatted without permission, responding aggressively when confronted by the owners of the lands on which they set up their camps. Sometimes, they stole. Almost without exception, they left behind mess and rubbish. Some encampments started wildfires, protesting their abuse by the blood families whose patrol units often treated them with contempt and violence.

Wehia understood why the border people were fearful and angry, but still . . . wildfires destroyed tracts of fen land and caused unhappiness amongst the fen folk. Wehia's holding was part of this community and her mother and aunts were critical of the border people. Fortunately, the buildings escaped damage. The border people were itinerant, but Wehia understood it was not solely by choice. That was part of their discontent. They felt that they had rights to parts of the fens and the blood families dealt with such claims most harshly, through their patrol units.

Wehia was filled with confusion when she thought about it. Were the border people's claims valid? She couldn't imagine anyone not wanting a permanent home, some stability. The border people's struggles might be solved if they were allowed to put down roots. Why didn't the blood families help them? She had tried to help them once . . . a long time ago, but she had failed . . .

At age six, Wehia had loved playing along the ore bogs. It was a sunny morning, close to Shovel-tide. The air was still crisp, the earth covered with faint frost, and Wehia had stayed too long indoors. The first chance she got, she ran outside and down along the river, sniffing the chilly air, reveling in the freedom of being outdoors. The sky was vast before her eyes. So was the land. The trees had begun to bud with light green, with the vines and tendrils starting to curl up sturdy trunks. Full of unspent energy, Wehia started to run.

She ran until she could run no more. Then, standing by the river, breathing hard, she turned her hot face to the breeze. The water, fanned into ripples, looked so cool. Tiny silver fish darted about in small schools. Wehia sighed with bliss. What freedom! She dreaded going back to the holding, where she must sit in a stuffy room to learn her letters.

A rustle startled her. Wehia looked up and met the gaze of a child, about her age, standing on the opposite bank. Wehia couldn't tell whether they were a girl or boy. Their thin face was covered with soot and dirt, which made the whites of their eyes startlingly bright. The child was dressed in a threadbare tunic and was barefoot. Their head was covered with a shock of light hair. The two stared at each other. Wehia thought the child looked cold—of course they were cold, dressed in rags—and hungry.

"Hello!" she called. Mother had warned her about "border people." This child must have been one of them. Wehia had always thought they looked harmless enough. Just hungry. *This* child looked hungry. Wehia, always ready for a meal, thought the child must surely wish for something to eat. "Hello! Do you want—Are you—hungry?" No response. But Wehia had decided. "Wait—stay there," she said. She ran back to the holding. The forge was busy—her mother and aunts working on their knives. She grabbed a loaf of fresh bread from the pantry. That would do!

When Wehia returned to the river's edge, the child was still there. Wehia wondered if she should throw the loaf over the narrow river—but what if it fell into the water? That would ruin it! Wehia considered the water . . . it was a shallow stretch—she could see the gravelly riverbed, the weeds growing between the stones. Perhaps she could just walk across . . .

"I brought you some bread," she called. "Food. Eat." She motioned putting her hand to her mouth. The child smiled, and the dirty face was suddenly transformed. Wehia had decided then and there that she would indeed cross the river with the loaf when she heard the sound of hooves. It was a patrol. She had seen them before, thundering down the lanes.

The child looked round, eyes wide open, like a

cornered animal. The small figure darted away, disappearing into the bushes. Wehia hugged the loaf and sighed. The patrol thundered by, five or six men on horseback. They did not stop and soon disappeared into the distance. Wehia wondered if she should wait—would the child return? But, after some minutes, Wehia decided that it was no good. She turned on her heels and ran home—where her mother caught her trying to sneak the loaf back into the bread bin. Later, Wehia had received a sharp scolding about "feeding strangers" and "helping border people who shouldn't be helped." Imagine wasting bread—precious bread! Wehia thought Mother sounded harsh. Even cruel and selfish. It was odd, coming from a woman who kept on telling Wehia to share whatever she had with her nieces and cousins.

Wehia tried to forget about the child. For a while, she dreamed about the waif. In her dreams, bread and fish were offered and received. It made her feel better. At least, she'd helped . . . in her dreams. She also tried crossing the icy-cold river once to look for the child. Unfamiliar brambles caught her skin, tore at her face. She got lost and was rescued by her aunts only after she had spent a shivery afternoon huddled under a moss-covered tree. She received a ferocious scolding from her mother: Wehia must never cross the river or speak to the border people.

"I want to help them!" protested Wehia tearfully, but

Mother was adamant. And withering.

However, even with the passing of time and an increasingly busy life, Wehia's memory of the child she had encountered did not dim. Furthermore, stories she heard about the border people added to the conflicting emotions that stirred in her heart. Her mother and aunts saw these people as nothing but a nuisance, but Wehia kept seeing the face of the child: the smile that had wiped out the hunger in their eyes, and the fear that had overwhelmed them when they had heard the patrol drawing near.

Surely those with enough to eat, a warm bed and clothes, and a roof over their heads, should do what they could for those who had nothing. If not the adults, then, at least the children—like the child she had met—deserved better than to be always cold, hungry, and afraid.

She often argued with her mother and her aunts about the border folk, but their vehemence silenced her all too quickly. She did not know enough about the situation to be able to state her case clearly; their declarations confused her because they seemed so certain, and she had only a memory and gut feelings to go on. Wehia felt helpless and frustrated and, somehow, guilty. She wondered at her family's apathy. Why didn't they care about those who were starving and poor? Why didn't they want to help? Was *she* the delusional one?

During the Months of the Knife and Saber, the t'Tolani fed the poor by opening their doors in the evening and giving them hot morani stew and bread, as well as clean blankets. Wehia and Geri joined the apprentices in handing out the food and blankets to the homeless. The recipients thanked them profusely. At festival times, the holding was a generous donor of food and ore to the Shrine. The Shrine, in turn, fed the transient and homeless. The thought that she was helping to some degree made Wehia feel slightly better about the whole situation with the beggars and border people. Yet it still didn't assuage the twisting guilt she felt in her stomach, the rioting sea of emotions in her heart.

While the t'Tolani holding prepared for Shovel-tide Eve, the spring cleaning all done, Wehia found some time to pore over her sword's design. It had to be perfect, so perfect that Hadana would be moved to grant her the permission to make it.

Wehia was pleased at the curves and flourishment of the hilt. They reminded her of the spread wings of a bird in flight. The blade she kept simple and clean so that its song would ring true at the end.

All she needed now was the Goddess's blessing and her aunt's approval, and work on the sword could start.

Excited, Wehia showed the design to Geri, who only praised the beauty of the sword pattern and said nothing further. Geri soon left the study room. Wehia wondered why she was in such a haste. Shovel-tide Eve chores? Wehia shrugged and was soon immersed in her sword's design again. But it was hard to concentrate, with so much activity going on. Some of the apprentices were cleaning the lanterns and drums in the courtyard in preparation for their journey to the Shrine. Their laughter came drifting into the study and Wehia, thinking she might take a break and join them, went to the study room door, only to see Geri hurry past, head bent, shoulders hunched, hands balled into fists. What had happened? The girl was headed to the forge, which caused Wehia to check her first impulse to follow. She must wait until the evening meal to find out what had upset her amal, her dearest heart.

But when they were seated and eating, it was obvious that Geri was not in the mood to share what was going on. Her face bore a scowl, something Wehia had not seen before, and she hardly gazed up from her bowl.

What was the reason for Geri's bad mood? Surely, she should have felt able to confide in Wehia, of all people. Wehia hesitated, wanting to know what was wrong, yet afraid that she would make things worse. Was it something she had done? Was Geri angry with her?

⊷⊢━━

On Shovel-tide Eve, Wehia Jirin t'Doniyat *ef* t'Tolani joined the forge women in a procession to the Shrine of the Goddess of Swords. They were clad in the color of the t'Tolani: sky blue. Their head shawls, which protected them from the elements, were also a shimmering blue. Their hands bore metal lanterns that swung slowly as they walked the steps to the Shrine. All the other holdings had their processions too, and the streams of pilgrims merged at the entrance of the Shrine in a brilliant sea of blue, green, brown, red, and yellow. Smaller holdings threaded in and out, their colors no less bright, their pride no less deep. It was a river of glowing lanterns. The sight took Wehia's breath away.

Wehia felt Geri's warm body beside her as they pressed towards the main Shrine, where the Goddess of Swords stood illuminated by a multitude of white candles, layer after layer of flickering flame. Her gloved hands held a sword, its tip turned downwards to the ground. Its design reminded Wehia of the Faith line type: elegant and beautiful. Her face was covered with a shawl, revealing only Her eyes. Generations of women and girls had hung trinkets on the walls: small, metal daggers winked in the light like stars; strings of tiny swords layered upon each other; necklaces of silver beads shaped like tiny serrated suns.

Farmer women brought their shovels to be blessed.

Fisher women brought their hooks and the blades they used to scale fish, to hang on the Goddess's fingers as they too sought Her protection. There were even bracelets of tiny, silver bells. At the feet of the marble Goddess were silver threads, twisted, joined and woven together by hands wishing for marital unions and pairings. The Shrine was huge, the space echoing with voices and songs. The ceiling seemed to go forward, a dome of blue, like the t'Tolani color but swirled with clouds. The priestesses beat their drums and shook their bells. Individual priestesses blessed throngs of women and girls. A few men stood out in the Shrine, dressed in their holdings' colors, but they were humble and retiring—farmhands from the orchards and plantations. They too sought the Goddess's blessings.

Hadana t'Tolani raised up the new year's wishes, symbolized in a bundle of steel strips, and sang out a chant to the Sword Goddess for good luck, and Her blessings on the holdings:

> *Lady, bless us!*
> *Lady, help us!*
> *Lady, be our guide!*
> *Lady, be our soul!*
> *Lady, be the sword that rings true!*

A white-clad priestess tied a silver thread around the steel strips and reverently carried the bundle away. Wehia didn't see where the priestess went. The Shrine was packed. Movement was hard. The air was thick with incense and the odors of many women packed together in a tight space.

Wehia reached for Geri's hands and the girl squeezed back. Wehia saw the eyes of the Goddess, calm and serene-looking. Would the Goddess bless them today? Would the Goddess bless the sword that she was going to make?

She whispered a prayer to the Goddess to bless her heart instead. She needed to be strong for both the sword and Geri. She also petitioned the Goddess so that She could facilitate the swift approval of her sword design. The eyes of the Goddess were impeccable and emotionless.

The t'Tolani procession threaded its way out of the main hall and Wehia breathed a sigh of relief, glad for the flow of cold air and the feeling of space around her. She suddenly yearned for the t'Doniyat private chapel, where a lone statue of the Goddess stood on the altar, adorned only with simple, silver trinkets and lit by one white candle. She would sometimes sit in the chapel, partly to escape her mother's nagging, partly to pray about things. The City's Shrine was imposing, filled with the City's power and might. A fitting companion to the Council

Hall. Everything *soared* in this City. Everything was so big, so grand. Wehia only thought of simple earth and wood, not marble, not glass.

"I wish to be out of this accursed robe!" Geri muttered, and Wehia giggled, relieved to see no trace of the girl's bad mood that had lingered for some days. The air was still cold, but their robes were warm, sticking to their skin, and, in the crush of the crowd, hot, heavy, and stifling. The procession flowed down the steps, passing latecomers in their colored robes. Wehia was careful to keep her lantern from swinging into other people's faces. When they reached the bottom of the Shrine's steps, her relief was overwhelming.

Later, when they had filed back into the t'Tolani holding, the news came—of fire. They all watched as soldiers from various blood families cantered down the streets, bearing arms. Their faces were grim. The fens were burning.

CHAPTER 9

THE SMELL OF SMOKE filled the City. It was wood fire, the result of swaths of forestland burning. Shovel-tide was spent airing the house and making sure the washing was kept indoors. People were subdued. The burning was out of season and had been blamed on either malicious vandals or the border people. Wehia cringed at the mention of these folk. The image of the border child resurfaced again in her mind. Why had the border people become such a thorn in her side? Councilors argued for sterner treaties with the border people. Outright wars had been waged before, and even in peace time, the truce between the border people and the City was fragile.

Wehia worried for her holding and how her family was coping. She wanted to go back to check on them. Geri cautioned her not to be so hasty. She was still in the midst of her apprenticeship and her sword design hadn't been approved by Hadana t'Tolani. With Geri, Wehia climbed up to the top of the t'Tolani building where the signal fire burned. Her heart suffered a sharp pang at the sight of the columns of smoke. They looked dark and ominous. The rest of the sky was a clear blue.

"They almost burned down where I live," Wehia fretted. "I have to go back."

"I understand, but you need to keep calm," Geri said. "I hear that it's not a large swath of land."

Wehia groaned in frustration. The talk on the streets was about border people, and that the brigands who often hunted along the roads were also border people, greedy for riches.

Even the gossip in the forge was all about them: Border people were troublemakers.

Border people stole livestock from the farms, as well as ripe fruits and grains from the orchards and plantations. Border people terrified children and caused nightmares. These vagrants disrupted the joy of Shovel-tide, which was supposed to be a week of gift-giving and merriment. The forge women shook their heads and grumbled. There should have been more control of the border folks' movements. They groused and grunted in approval at the news that Council troops had been sent to quell the unrest and stop the fires before valuable tracts of land were razed.

A mood of disquiet filled the forge. Everybody grew irritable. It was hard to concentrate with all the smoke and complaints about border people. The forge was stifling with the smell of wood smoke. It got into throats and noses, causing soreness and itchy ears.

During this period, women usually gave their friends small gifts of necklaces and bracelets made of tiny shovels and bells. That year was no different. They were determined to celebrate Shovel-tide, no matter what. In recent times, it was not just shovels, but delicate rings, thin daggers, slender arrows. Geri gave Wehia such a necklace, with filigree silver rings. She had made it herself. In return, Wehia slid a silver ring on Geri's finger. This too was part of Shovel-tide because promises were made during the Month of the Shovel and seeds were planted for the future.

Hadana hoped to dispel the bad mood in the forge. She encouraged celebration and merrymaking at the holding. The t'Tolani drank homemade wine made from fen rice, sang, and danced together, the frame drums keeping time with their hearts. Hadana joined in, and Wehia danced a little, but her mind was still stuck on her family. She could not forget the fires. Her family's bog lay directly between shrubland and border. Was everyone safe? If not, she would surely have heard by now, but then what if things were really bad and they could not send word?

Again, she thought about the child she had met. The child who would have been a young—woman? man?—now. What did they make of all this? Were they as bewildered as she was?

"A careless hand," one of the t'Tolani women said loudly, her face ruddy with rice wine. "A careless hand tossing a lit match. Even an empty glass bottle can spark off fire."

Her friends nodded at her words. Wehia glanced quickly at her aunt, whose lips were thin and demeanor strict and unsmiling, a looming thunder head with flickers of lightning.

"Careless talk by idle tongues." Hadana t'Tolani spoke, and that group of women fell silent. "Let the Council deal with the fire," the forge mistress continued, softening her tone. "We are simple folk. Speculation can easily turn into rumor and vice versa. We cannot afford to add to false words."

"I apologize, my lady." The red-faced t'Tolani woman inclined her head, tipsy no longer. Hadana was beloved and highly respected. The women listened to her.

Hadana smiled then, the darkness dissipated, and she was beautiful. "We can all easily fall into a trap of thinking too much. Come, Sister, let's dance once more. We bring in good fortune this Shovel-tide!"

The frame drums began to beat again and the women linked hands, forming a circle. The dining hall rang with their laughter as they danced.

The apprentices sat at their table, watching the senior women dance. Wehia admired the authority Hadana commanded, and the respect and loyalty the women felt was immense. Her own mother too was held in high esteem by the forge women she commanded, but Hadana had something more. She really was like a queen, a goddess—fearsome yet also inspiring love.

"She is dazzling," Wehia murmured to Geri.

"That she is," agreed her companion. "She runs the forge and the family business like my grandmother before her. She is fierce, but she is also kind. And she listens to the women. We often think she is just all plate armor, protecting a tender heart."

"Does she really have a tender heart?" Wehia raised her eyebrows. "She's all steel inside. Hard!"

Geri laughed. "She simply hides her heart well."

They overheard some of the other women, huddled together near them, still gossiping about border people. Fortunately, Hadana was with her senior forge women and did not notice.

"We have kin who live in the borderlands too." Geri's voice dropped to a conspiratorial whisper. "Many swordsmith holdings have kin living as border people. The fight is over land and who gets to have the land. It is complicated. I don't like it."

"Nor do I," Wehia agreed. Her mother had once hinted that they had relatives living amongst the border folk. They were separated from the family only by land rights laws, customs, and pride. Mostly pride? Wehia wondered why they had ended estranged from the rest of the family.

"In the end, we are all flesh and blood." Geri shrugged and poured more warm plum cider into their wooden mugs. "The Goddess of Swords made all of us different, and isn't that a good thing? Yet not when the differences separate us, cut into us, and make us angry."

Wehia was reminded of the egg-slicer they used back at the t'Doniyat holding. It was made of fine, thin, metal wires. It sliced into peeled hardboiled eggs, separating the eggs into neat sections. Wehia knew that what separated border, fen, and City folk was not merely thin, silver wires. Between just fen and City, the gulf was deep, even though there might not have been animosity. And what of the border people? Was the problem that they fell through the cracks, dismissed and disregarded, because the fen and City folk were too preoccupied with their own affairs?

"You would make a good councilor," Wehia teased Geri. "You speak with eloquence."

Geri's cheeks bloomed rose pink. "I am only of swordsmith stock. I could not be a Council member even if I wanted to be one."

"Our common ancestress made the Council sword!" Wehia retorted. "She sat at the Council table too."

"Those days are in the past. We are no longer eligible for Council positions. We merely make their swords and daggers for the blood duels and other arguments they create out of nothing. We make trinkets for them so that they can while away their free time."

"But swordsmith holdings are respected, aren't we?"

"We are." Geri nodded. "The Council sword rests in the middle of City Hall, broken as it is. It's a reminder of the past."

Wehia took in these words and nursed them in her heart. Would their ancestress be ashamed that the Council sword still remained shattered? Why didn't anyone repair the sword? She shook her head, determined to enjoy the festivities. Soon, the plum cider was gone from their mugs. Warm with cider and companionship, Geri drew a protesting Wehia to the dance circle. They spun around, giggling, and, for a moment, Wehia was joyful. However, she grew weary quickly and her mind wandered back to her sword.

While the Shovel-tide festivities continued into the night, she made an excuse to leave the dining hall. Geri let her go. The kitchen staff had brewed hot fen-free tea for those who wanted to cleanse their palate. With a mug of the astringent beverage, Wehia slipped back into the forge's study room. The silence welcomed her like warm, loving arms. Her sword called to her. *Fire Heart*—she would be called "Fire Heart"!

Wehia lost herself in Fire Heart's design and the song the sword sang to her—even on crinkly parchment paper and manuscript ink. Her sword was not going to be just a reminder of times past. It would be present and *glorious*.

A true Faith sword. Belief, clarity, steel.

⊣————

Later, Wehia made her way to the top of the building. The cool wind buffered her, bringing with it the hint of wood fire. She stared out into the distance, across the City, across the sea of lights. Wehia could still make out the faint columns of smoke. They were a billowing white against the darkness. She tried to convince herself once more that they were far away from where her holding was. Wehia whispered a quick prayer to the Sword Goddess to keep her family safe.

CHAPTER 10

FOR A FEW DAYS, while the City marked Shovel-tide week with the shining brightness of fireworks and the thunderous claps of firecrackers, Wehia worked on the design of her sword. She added the last few flourishes on the hilt with dark ink, the swirls surfacing like a flicker of light in murky bog water. "Fire Heart," she whispered. *Fire Heart.* The sword had the basic shape and style of her kin; the blade long, slowly tapering to a fine tip, straight and double-edged. It would have a double fuller, like Cold Steel. The swords would be, in essence, sisters. The blade would bear her name and the marks of her maker's holding, and that of the t'Tolani.

"You will rise up, like a flame, like the fire that dances along the bog," Wehia sang to the sword-to-be. "Like the sun, you will shine." *Fire Heart,* she repeated to herself. *Fire Heart.* She sang the name, the sounds of it, the syllables and vowels of it, into the design, tracing its outline while the words came forth from her mouth and her mind. She made sure the design glowed brightly, in her mind's eye, the edges shimmering a white-blue—not surprising, as the foundation would be part t'Tolani and their style was an integral part of the sword. She sang and sang, until the sword's voice was loud and clear, crystal transparent and piercing like a tuning fork.

Later, she stood at her window, watching the last of the night's fireworks light up the sky. The sight of the golden sparkles filled her heart with hope and anticipation.

"It's done," Wehia said. "It's finally done."

Now she had to convince Hadana.

Unfortunately, Hadana wasn't around to look at the design and approve its making. She had been called away to another holding—the t'Mallah needed her expertise and advice.

The forge still buzzed with industry, under the watchful eye of her deputy forge mistress, Rika, a dour woman who hovered constantly, finding fault with everything and everyone.

Geri wasn't around, either. As a trusted and capable senior apprentice, she had been asked to accompany her aunt to the t'Mallah holding. The forge was a cold and heartless place without her cheerful presence. Wehia reached up to touch the necklace that Geri had given her and felt reassured. Rika had set Wehia numerous tasks, all menial, so she was kept busy from day till night. She poured water for the senior forge women, carried the ore from the store, and cleaned the crucibles at the end of the day. It was just like the days when she had yet to win the forge's trust, when Hadana had been testing her for grit and resilience. Wehia simply shouldered it and moved on, her sword's design aglisten in her mind and heart. She forced herself to smile and thought of daily joys in her life. It made working under Rika so much easier. Hadana—and Geri—would soon be back.

In her room, Wehia practiced with Cold Steel, listening to the muffled sounds of the City at the end of Shovel-tide. More fireworks and laughter from the fine balconies and rooftops. Many of the blood families threw grand parties, the ladies and their lords entertaining their finely-dressed guests with exquisite food and expensive wines. Some made it a big show, to plant seeds in half-turned soil, to symbolize the start of a new year. Some would even plant saplings, which they grew in their private steam-powered greenhouses. The printing press would make a fuss about these overt shows of wealth and publish glowing reports in breathless tones. Wehia generally ignored them. Breathing, working on her drills, concentrating on her balance mattered most. She had spent too much time in the forge. She needed to regain her footing.

The weight of Cold Steel felt so right in her hands. It might have felt the same in her great-grandmother's. From what her mother had said, Great-grandmother had been quite a fighter when she'd run the holding as the matriarch. She had fought opponents even at seventy and had soundly beaten them. Wehia wasn't sure why the sword had been left to languish in the armory. Why had her great-grandmother put it there? They'd been longsword makers and had obviously fought using their creations. Perhaps Great-grandmother had wanted Cold Steel to be found by one of her great-granddaughters or nieces. Bloodlines had to be continued, carried into the next generation. Wehia wanted to press her mother once more about the reason why they had stopped making longswords.

If Great-grandmother had made longswords, why was their holding now a minor one?

She swung the blade, listening to the metal hum: Cold Steel's own song. Wehia felt so alive. She wanted Geri to see this aspect of her, holding Cold Steel and practicing with it. Geri had seen the sword and held it, but her heart was into the making of daggers and related blades. Geri practiced with her own dagger and Wehia loved watching her when she went through the drills. She made it look effortless.

Each day, after her practice session, Wehia would walk up to the building's rooftop to see if the fires had stopped. She was still worried about her holding's safety. Part of her wanted to go back to check on her family. That day, she was relieved to see that the columns of wood smoke had dissipated. The gossip about border people had also, thankfully, died down. She shuddered at the thought of the destruction left behind by the fires. Wehia could hear the laughter of Shovel-tide merry makers. People were playing music, singing and dancing. It struck her that the City folk were unconcerned about the fires.

Hadana would return. Hadana would approve of her design. Wehia kept these thoughts fresh in her head, even when she lay down and slept, the sounds of fireworks and riotous parties fading into the night.

Hadana stayed at the t'Mallah holding for two nights beyond the eight days she had set aside. It had taken longer than anticipated to resolve the matter that they had been called to attend to. The commission by Lady Barita was challenging: a filigree sword that had to be both functional and ornamental. The t'Mallah was out of their depth with this commission and rued that the t'Tolani would have to take over. However, the deadline was approaching and Hadana confirmed that they shouldn't have delayed their decision. That was Hadana: firm and stern, when the situation demanded it.

Meanwhile, back at the t'Tolani holding, Rika set Wehia more tasks. Wehia kept her mouth shut and completed the jobs, one by one. It was at dawn on the first day of the new week when the door of the t'Tolani holding was flung open, letting in a gust of cold air. Hadana, in her brilliant blue, stepped in, her eyes flashing like spring lightning, with Geri, in a similar robe, following meekly. Hadana held a cloth-wrapped bundle in her arms, cradling it lovingly.

"Stoke up the forge, start the fires raging," Hadana roared. "The fool t'Mallah are cowardly and have waited too long. Women, my sisters, we will show them what we can do!"

For two days and nights, the forge burned brightly and roared loudly. The fires were kept going. The t'Mallah's delay was a big mistake. The rest of the filigree sword was left undone, the design unraveling under pressure. Hadana deemed it too ambitious, with many unnecessary flourishes at the cross guard. It had become too unwieldly. Aided by her most senior and experienced women, Hadana re-melted the metal and hammered the glowing mass into the shape of a blade once more, her arms gleaming with sweat, her hair tied up.

While the sword's blade was worked on, Amira, one of the senior forge women, was told to begin making the hilt. Lady Barita loved gems, and so the sword was to have myriad gems studded along the pommel. Amira had vast knowledge of, and a passion for, gem stones. She also possessed a gift of designing settings that brought out the best in the gems she selected for any project. She sat down and worked, picking choice gems from her collection with fine tweezers.

"Come, apprentices," Hadana called out and the girls came obediently. "Come, see how the sword is sharpened."

She started the whetting wheel with her foot and carefully placed the blade's edge on the spinning wheel. Sparks flew. Hadana chuckled, not minding the sparks. "This sword will be pretty and dangerous at the same time," she told the girls. "Lady Barita duels, even in her finery."

Wehia had no idea who Lady Barita was. But she remembered the name so that she could avoid this lady of the blood in the future.

"Come, Wehia," Hadana said later. "You make the scabbard. I am sure you know how to make a scabbard, hmm?"

Wehia gasped, feeling a weight settle on her shoulders.

"Do not tarry. When you are done, show Amira—

the scabbard has gems on it too. Quickly, because we are running on a deadline."

So Wehia got to work without another word. It usually took an eight-day or more to make a scabbard, and Wehia pushed down her impatience and focused on her task. She made the scabbard from apple-wood and polished it until it gleamed under the light. She had done this many times, in the forge of her holding, as they made ornamental daggers. Making a longer scabbard wasn't difficult for her. She made sure the edges were smooth and that the blade was able to rest in it, snug and secure. Once she was done, she handed the scabbard to Amira.

By the end of the third eight-day, a day before the final deadline, the filigree sword was complete. A final cleaning and buffing was done, until the ornamental sword shone and the gems lit up the forge like a sea of stars. With ceremony, the t'Tolani proudly presented it to Lady Barita, who received the sword with utmost delight and made the promise of future patronage—she already had another design in mind! The t'Mallah were disgraced and nobody would hear of them until years later when they redeemed themselves by making an exquisite dagger for a lord.

And now the work was over. *Finally*, Wehia thought. *Finally.*

That evening, she took her sword design to Hadana, who was sitting by the fire in her private study. It was still cold and the forge mistress often rested in her favorite chair, a cup of fen tea next to her. She nodded at Wehia, who stood, breathless, and daring not to breathe. Hadana t'Tolani donned her reading glasses and peered closely at the design, the curves and the flourishes, the song swirling, embedded like the sword's heart, and remained silent for a long time.

When Wehia's heart had almost reached its bursting point, Hadana gently placed the design on the table and lifted the cup of tea to her lips. She sipped once, twice, before resting it on her lap.

"The sword is beautiful," Hadana said. "And that's the truth. It is a beautiful design."

Wehia exhaled slowly and softly, her heart beating painfully in her chest.

"Well . . . and why do you show this to me, Wehia?"

"Aunt—I-I wish to make this sword."

"And so you will . . . when I say you are ready."

"Aunt, I am ready. Look at my drawing."

"It is a fine drawing, but . . . it is a drawing, not a sword. What does it show me except that you have a dream?"

"It is more than a dream!" cried Wehia. "She sang to me and bade me make her."

Hadana stared at her. "So . . ." She nodded. "I am glad that you hear her. Still, the song means nothing if you cannot carry it—with skill, and experience. To be sure, it would be a beautiful sword, if I let you make it, but . . . will it rest on a solid foundation? If you make this thing of beauty, will it last?"

Wehia's eyes burned with tears. "Aunt—"

"My dear child, daughter of my second cousin far removed . . . why do you push so hard? What I am asking of you is not unusual. I am not punishing you, or testing you. Like any other apprentice, you must be patient; you must realize that I know what I am about. If I say you are not ready, then you are not."

"But I am not just *any* apprentice!"

Hadana's eyes widened at Wehia's words and a frown creased her brow, but only fleetingly, as laughter got the better of her. She threw her head back and laughed, rocking in her chair.

"Aunt, I mean it," said Wehia, encouraged by the fact that Hadana was not angry. "I know I am ready. I have made knives and daggers for my mother's holding and—"

"Knives and daggers are not swords, Wehia," said Hadana, although she still smiled.

"I will be careful; I will do what you say," pleaded Wehia.

Hadana snorted. "Yet you will not listen when I say to wait."

"I know I can do this, Aunt Hadana."

The forge mistress said nothing for a long while. She

gazed into the fire thoughtfully and finally she said, "Wehia, you must understand that swords are not just beautiful objects. They are not just pretty pictures on parchment. They have a purpose. Just one tiny mistake and they are not swords anymore. They cannot have flaws. Flaws are fatal. They mean death . . . or worse. Do you understand, Wehia?"

"Y-Yes, Aunt. I know this. I will be careful. I will take as much time as necessary to make this sword, but I want to begin."

Hadana sighed. "You must think hard about the making. Think of the metal composition. What kind of alloys do you plan to use? What amounts? Check the sword's length. Is it based on the design recorded in the book of swords? Use the book well—it is there to help you. Think of each part of your sword. Each part has to be perfect, to make a perfect whole. Ask the forge women for advice—do not be proud. Listen to what I have to say. Wehia . . ."

"Yes, Aunt?"

"Wehia, I want you to examine your motives. *Why* do you want to make this sword? What is the rush? How do you know you are ready? Are you free from distractions; are you strong enough to last through all the troubles and doubts that will come your way?"

Hadana patted Wehia's hand kindly. The hard exterior of the t'Tolani forge mistress fell away. A gentler, softer expression settled upon the holding's mistress's face. "Wehia, if you have been in this business for a long time, you know that you cannot give up. Your mother knows this. All forge mistresses know this. Just because your patron criticizes you, or your design is flawed, you must not run away from it all. You will not last as a forge mistress with such thinking. We all learn from our mistakes, from trial and error, from circumstances beyond our control. Believe it or not, we have had many commissions that failed. Commissions that looked pretty in the beginning but failed when they were put to the test. Things will go wrong—count on it. I want you to make your heart strong enough for this undertaking."

"Aunt—"

Hadana held up her hand. "Now go. Go and think of all I have said. Ask yourself the questions I have asked you. Why now? Why not wait? Are you ready? Is your resolve unshakeable? Will you be easily discouraged or distracted? Think about everything." Hadana smiled, a quick flash of even, white teeth. "Then come back to me tomorrow." She handed the parchment paper back to Wehia.

Wehia nodded before inhaling slowly. Her lungs filled with a growing hope. Determination steeled her heart.

CHAPTER II

WEHIA COULDN'T SLEEP. She sat down, charcoal stick in hand, and began sketching the different components of a sword again. On paper and in her head, she drew the parts that formed the pommel, the grip, the cross guard, the tang, and the blade.

Was she ready? Yes, she was! She felt it, deep in her heart.

What was the harm in waiting? The truth was she could have waited—it would not have killed her. Wehia acknowledged that there was no reason to hurry, except . . . why *should* she wait if she was ready?

She could not really explain why she felt so deeply about making Fire Heart. It was as if the sword were calling to her, telling her not to wait. She felt the summon in her heart and she heard the song in her head, all the time.

Nothing would distract her from the task. There was nothing she wanted more than to make Fire Heart. What could possibly make her turn away from it? She knew it would not be easy, and she knew she would spend long hours on the sword, that she would have to put all her attention on it, that she might make mistakes and there might be things she would have to do and re-do until they were just right. No distractions . . . no distractions—Wehia hesitated but then shook her head vehemently. No, *no* distractions, not even Geri. Geri knew how important this was to her. She would understand Wehia's preoccupation. And it would not be forever. The sword would eventually be made and then, Wehia would make it up to Geri.

She inhaled deeply and expelled her breath slowly, willing herself to be calm. She had to be focused, with nothing clouding her heart, nothing distracting her. She needed to believe in herself.

Wehia nodded. She knew she could do it.

"Aunt," Wehia called out to Hadana t'Tolani. It was still an hour before dawn, but the forge mistress was already awake, checking the forge before the day's work started. "Aunt, a moment please, if you have time."

Hadana frowned, squinting slightly before she smiled. "Ahh, it's you, Wehia."

"I have thought about everything," Wehia said. "I have asked myself what you told me to."

"And so . . ." Hadana smiled grimly.

"Aunt, I do not want to wait because . . . I *feel* I am ready. My sword is waiting for me—she wants me to make her now. I am impatient, yes, but my sword is more impatient than I am. I don't just *want* to start making her. I *need* to. And *she* needs me to start making her."

Hadana nodded. "So you have told me once before. But you know I may let you give into this impulse, I may say, 'Make your sword,' and you will have to then show great patience. You can no longer rush and push. You know you cannot do that to your sword."

"I know, Aunt."

"And, Wehia, what about your heart? Is your heart ready? Is your heart clear? Are you free from distractions? Will you shatter at the hint of stress?"

Wehia looked solemnly at her aunt. "I am ready."

"The process will be long and tedious. I want you to be strong—like the tang in your sword, your heart must not break. Are you sure you are truly ready?"

"Yes. I am ready."

Hadana was unsmiling, but her expression was gentle. She nodded slowly. "Very well . . . then, we begin at the start of the Hammer."

⊢———

"Wehia!"

Geri's voice stopped Wehia before she entered the forge. Her heart was still singing, still full of joy. It felt as if it wanted to burst from sheer exhilaration. She was finally going to make Fire Heart!

"A moment, if you are not busy," Geri said. Wehia was taken aback by her amal's appearance. Her eyes were red and swollen, her skin blotchy, and the girl was hunched over, her arms held crossed over her abdomen.

"Geri. What's wrong?"

"I—" Geri pulled Wehia into the silence of the courtyard. Shovel-tide marked the return of life in the garden. The vines budded a vivid, light green, and jeweled shapes darted back and forth, wings buzzing—the hummers had come back to make their nests in the vines and nooks. New life was happening everywhere.

"Geri, *what's happened?*" repeated Wehia.

"I-I ha-have to tell you, Wehia, I didn't want to worry you—I thought I was overreacting and the—*it* would go away, but . . . Wehia, I can't. I can't—"

"Geri, what is it? Shh . . . Look, take a deep breath—" Wehia held Geri firmly by her shoulders. "Just breathe for a second. Breathe. There . . . all right? Now, start again. Tell me."

Geri shook her head and closed her eyes tight. "Wehia"—the name came forth almost a wail—"Oh, Wehia . . . Lord Marik . . . he has asked me to marry him—

except I don't think he really wants to marry me—and I can't—"

"*What?*"

Wehia's heart plunged from its lofty height, all thoughts of making Fire Heart disappearing in an instant. Cold fingers wrapped themselves round her throat and squeezed. Her hands slipped off Geri's shoulders and she said slowly, very slowly, "Who . . . Who is Lord Marik?"

Geri's face crumpled, her eyes filling with tears. She leaned forward, pressing her forehead against Wehia's chest. "Wehia . . ."

"No, Geri! Geri, tell me properly—*who* is Lord Marik?"

"Oh, do not sound so angry, Wehia."

"*Geri* . . ."

"He—He is the son of L-Lord Vess. They are a blood family."

"And how do you know him, Geri?"

"We have made swords and daggers for him and his friends. They have come here w-with commissions. That is how I—How he came to know of me."

Wehia flinched. "Do you care for this man, Geri?"

"No!" Geri's look of anguish assured Wehia somewhat, but still, the icy hand constricted her throat.

"The first time he came here . . . It was months before you arrived. I was with Aunt Hadana when she received him and his friend. I did not pay much attention to him, but they had brought a dagger to show our aunt—it was beautiful. You know how I love daggers, Wehia—I think that is why Aunt Hadana had me with her. She knew I would love to see the dagger they brought. They wanted us to make two daggers like it . . ." Geri sighed.

"Go on," said Wehia, her voice very low.

"He came again soon after, with two other friends. There were more commissions—a sword and two daggers. And then . . ."

"Geri, just tell me."

"He—He wrote me a letter."

"What did he say in the letter, Geri?" To her own ears, Wehia sounded like a stranger.

"Wehia, I *swear*, I do not care for him."

"What did he say, Geri?"

"I-I don't remember his exact words. I burned it. I did not want it. I didn't want his attentions. I do not want his attentions."

"So he said he wanted you, Geri?"

"He—He asked me what I felt for him—whether I could ever lo-love him, whether I could imagine being Lady Marik. I did not answer. I burned the letter."

"Obviously, that didn't deter him."

"He started sending me gifts."

"*What* did he send you?"

"I don't know! I sent them all back. I did not open them."

Wehia sighed. Her hands returned to Geri's shoulders. She squeezed them. "Geri . . ."

"Wehia, you must believe me—I want nothing to do with this man. I do not care for him. Not at all."

"Geri . . . I believe you, but . . . how is it that he is asking you to marry him? How is it that he mistakes your indifference for interest—surely, he doesn't wish to marry someone who does not care for him."

"The third time he came, he wanted to commission a rapier for himself. He asked for me to be present, but I told our aunt I was ill. She was surprised that he'd asked for me—I saw it in her face when she told me I should be there to receive him. I said nothing, though. When the hour came, I told Aunt Hadana that I had to go to my room, that I felt sick. I did feel sick. I did not want to see him! But—" Geri shook her head vigorously and tears spilled down her flushed cheeks. "He—He told our aunt his intentions. And h-he told her that I had agreed to be his wife."

"*What?* He *lied?*"

"He lied, Wehia. I told Aunt Hadana so, but she made light of it, as if she didn't believe me. She even teased me for being bashful, as if I had denied my feelings because I was embarrassed. Shortly after that, you came to us, Wehia. Wehia, I liked you the moment I saw you. I knew at once. I do not like Lord Marik."

Wehia gathered Geri into her arms and held her

close. Her dearest amal was trembling.

"If you don't wish to marry him, simply say so. I don't see the problem or why you are so upset."

"Oh, Wehia." Geri began to cry again. "Wehia, Lord Marik came again, not long ago, with his friends, and Aunt Hadana insisted I receive them with her. After the meeting, she left us alone in the main hall—he must have requested it, and she agreed. I didn't know what to do—I couldn't refuse—my aunt would have been furious and seen it as unforgivable, a loss of face. He—He said he meant to marry me. He said he had his heart set on me and that Aunt Hadana had given her approval—"

"Geri, no!"

"Later, he wrote to our aunt and asked if his father should make a formal offer of marriage. She summoned me then and I told her I didn't love him—didn't even know him, really. She—"

The cold hand of fear tightened around Wehia's heart. She swallowed. "What did she say, Geri?"

"She asked me to consider how the marriage would benefit the holding."

"*WHAT?!*"

"She said that there are times when we have to do what is best for our family and our business. She asked me if I thought I had the makings of a forge mistress and if so, if I could show her what I was prepared to do."

"I can't believe . . . Geri, you said she had a tender

heart—you have just described someone without *any* heart. How could she suggest that you marry a man you don't know or care for, just for the sake of . . . *what?* Patronage? Favors granted?"

Geri wrung her hands. "She—She said that if there was a formal proposal and I refused, it would be a loss of face for our holding."

Wehia turned violently away from her and began to pace. "What is this woman? Can she really be so cold? And Lord Vess—would he make a formal offer of marriage to someone who does not wish to be his son's wife? There is no such thing as forced marriages in Metakse. Both parties must agree before a formal offer is made. Our aunt must know that, and I'm certain Lord Vess does too."

"That is the case, in theory. Marriage alliances are often made between families without consulting the actual couple."

Wehia stood stock-still. "What are you saying? That you will go along with it?"

"No! I am saying I don't know what to do. I truly don't know—"

"You—What do you mean, Geri? You will refuse him, of course."

"I *have* refused him. But you know as well as I do that when it comes to the formal offer, it is my aunt who must refuse. It is not up to me then."

Wehia's shoulders sagged. "You should have told me sooner."

"I know."

"I can't—Geri! I will *not* stand by and see you forced to marry this man. It is wrong. What Aunt Hadana said is wrong! If she accepts on your behalf—Goddess forgive her if she does—" Wehia's gorge rose. Rage burned. "She should be protecting you, not making you feel like you owe it to the holding to form an alliance with a blood family."

Geri said nothing, but fresh tears had begun to fall.

"Is Lord Vess an honorable man?"

"What? I-I don't know. I have only heard that his son does not live up to the family's good name."

"If he is an honorable man, he will not make the formal offer. If he knows you are not willing to marry Lord Marik, he will *not* make the offer." Wehia gazed at Geri. "I would tell him. If Lord Marik refuses to listen, then his father must be told."

"Oh, Wehia . . . Perhaps Lord Vess knows and does not care."

"Then he should be challenged! Even if families allow it, forced marriages are illegal in Metakse. If Aunt Hadana will not protect you, as she should, from the attentions of a man you do not love, and from his family, then I will have to. *I* will challenge Lord Vess."

Geri began to protest. "No! Wehia, you cannot!

Challenging blood family members is illegal!"

"I bet he has never been challenged by a woman," Wehia laughed.

⚔

Wehia stared at Fire Heart, the sword design shimmering on the parchment. *I must be strong like you. You must be strong like me. Our hearts must be strong. They must beat together.*

Geri had to be saved.

The necklace around Wehia's neck felt heavy. She had made a promise. Promises shouldn't be broken.

Oh, Fire Heart. I want to make you, make you real.

But she . . . she *had* to protect Geri.

⚔

Wehia decided to send an anonymous summons to Lord Vess: *To Lord Vess, Meet me at Pier 14. We have a matter to settle involving your son, Lord Marik. We will duel, if necessary.*

Geri protested vehemently, but it was too late to stop the messenger.

"It's foolhardy—do you want to be killed? Please, *please*, have more sense!"

"He's not going to force you into marriage!" Wehia snarled. Cold Steel was solid in her hands. She tested the sword's weight. Her weapon was ready. She was ready.

"Think about your sword!" Geri pleaded. "You made a promise—to make your sword. Please, please, *please* calm down and think about your sword! I-I want you to be unharmed. This is so dangerous!"

Wehia wavered. Her heart wavered. It hurt, being pulled in two different directions. *Oh, why did it hurt so much?* Seeing Geri's tears strengthened her resolve. She couldn't tolerate the idea of Geri being forced into a loveless union. Hadana t'Tolani might kill her in the end. So might her mother. But Wehia just had to protect Geri. Hadana wouldn't even protect her own niece. What kind of aunt was she?

"I will go." She kissed Geri lightly on the lips. Geri shook her head sadly, knowing nothing she said would change Wehia's mind.

CHAPTER 12

PIER 14 WAS DESERTED when Wehia arrived, clad from head to toe in t'Tolani blue. She had never walked along the docks alone at night before. It was very still. This late, the piers and docks next to the River Verru were silent, the boats and tugs all covered, the pilots asleep. Her footsteps sounded deafening. She concentrated on stepping more lightly.

A chill enveloped the City. There was no fog. Wehia gazed up briefly at the signal fires. They rivaled the stars in brightness. The stars looked different at Shovel-tide's end: the Anvil now tilted east, the Forge south. One single star, the tip of the Sword of Spring, shone brightly.

She controlled her breathing, moving into a light meditative trance, still aware of her surroundings, but now going inward.

A figure walked up. Dressed all in black, it was like a shadow come to life. A typical blood family strategy: wearing black to mask their identity and turn them into anonymous duelists. Even their face was masked, showing only their eyes, but, in the darkness, she couldn't see them clearly.

"My lord," she said, and the figure halted. The man had a dancer's grace. He moved on the balls of his feet.

"A woman?" The voice was deep.

"Yes." Wehia spoke, proud with righteous anger, her courage filling her up like forge fire. "A woman."

The man removed his face mask. "I am Lord Vess." He bowed.

"I am Wehia Jirin t'Doniyat *ef* t'Tolani." Wehia was surprised that her voice didn't shake. "I come to fight for Geri Shaara *ef* t'Tolani's honor."

"Geri *ef* t'Tolani?" Lord Vess frowned. "I have no feud with the t'Tolani. You are an honorable swordsmith holding. And, lest you forget, we are not supposed to fight."

Wehia held her sword in front of her. "Lord Marik wants to marry Geri Shaara. He says you will make a formal offer. But Geri Shaara does not want to marry your son. Will you still make the offer? If you do, Hadana t'Tolani will probably accept. Will you sentence Geri t'Tolani to a life she does not want?'

Even in the dim light, Wehia could see the man's face darken.

"I would never make a formal proposal for the hand of a woman who does not wish to join my family," said Lord Vess. "What is Marik playing at—he has not even mentioned this girl, much less that she is not willing to marry him. He knows I would not approve. Forcing a woman into marriage . . . that practice has been forbidden for at least a hundred years. My son is a fool," he growled.

Wehia could only nod.

"And you came to fight for her honor?" Lord Vess's craggy face broke into a smile then. "I suspect *you* are not just cousins. You are very brave to challenge a blood to an honor duel. There's not much to fight for at the moment. I could *wring* his neck on your behalf."

Wehia's bravado fizzled out. The realization slowly dawned on her that she had been foolish. Her actions could have dire consequences.

But . . .

"Lady Wehia," Lord Vess said, his voice kind. "I know that you came for a duel. Your heart was geared towards it. Yet I feel that you are not ready. Your heart is *somewhere else*. The night is pleasant; the air is sweet. The stars shine brightly tonight. We can have a practice fight, to allay your fears and give you something to talk about later."

"'Practice fight'?" Wehia blurted out, feeling more the fool now.

"You brought your sword, a *Faith* sword," Lord Vess said with an appreciative whistle. "I use a sword who is cousin to it."

And so, they bantered into the night. Lord Vess's

sword belonged to the Truth line, a type that resembled the Faith swords in overall design, but with a narrower blade. They fought lightly.

Vess showed Wehia various fighting stances and sword strokes. For any onlookers and stragglers walking past the pier, it appeared that a duel was in progress. Duels were so commonplace in the City that most onlookers would walk away after observing for a little while.

When it was time to go, when the Anvil slid farther east and the Forge virtually disappeared into the horizon, Lord Vess bowed once more.

"Go back to your holding, Lady Wehia *ef* t'Tolani. I respect the swordsmith holdings for their integrity. Your sense of honor cheers me, though now I need to administer justice to my own son. There will be no formal offer of marriage, rest assured."

"Thank you . . . Lord Vess," Wehia said.

"Let's forget this meeting ever happened. Promise me that you will never do this again, Lady Wehia—for your own good." Lord Vess smiled and Wehia nodded slowly.

He donned his mask again, bowed, and disappeared into the night. Wehia's heart was full of questions. She had not expected to be treated with such kindness, such compassion. Not by a blood. She pulled up her mask and headed back to the holding.

The blue t'Tolani door was open. Hadana t'Tolani stood arms akimbo, framed by the light of the holding. Her eyes burned with anger.

Wehia's fear rushed back, filling her lungs.

"Where in the nine hells did you go?"

"Aunt—"

"Do not just stand there!" Hadana cried. "Enter— *NOW!*"

Wehia hurried in, glad for the warmth the courtyard provided. Hadana slammed the door shut.

"Now tell me why you slipped out of the house in the middle of the night," Hadana hissed.

It was now or never.

"I went to fight. For Geri's honor. I challenged Lord Vess."

Hadana's jaw fell, but she quickly recovered her composure. "You went to fight for my niece's honor? Are you a fool? It's illegal to challenge a blood family!"

"Who cares? Someone needed to speak for Geri. She doesn't want to marry Lord Marik and he said his father would be making a formal offer."

"It was none of your concern, Wehia. How dare you interfere!"

"I had to do *something*. You should have backed Geri up. I cannot believe that you suggested she accept the proposal. Well, I have resolved the matter. There will be no formal offer of marriage. And, incidentally, Lord

Marik never mentioned his intentions to his father. He was probably toying with Geri. And with you!"

Hadana's face fell.

"You should have protected Geri. She didn't want to marry him, but you didn't care. You are . . . *selfish*—"

"Go to your room!" roared Hadana.

Wehia took a step back. "I'm sorry, Aunt, but—"

"GO TO YOUR ROOM!"

Hadana's shout echoed through the building. It also destroyed the last shreds of Wehia's bravado.

Wehia brushed past Hadana. Once in her room, she threw herself on her bed, crying. Her pillow soaked up all her tears and Cold Steel was the only witness to her pain.

The truth surfaced a day or two later. Geri whispered it, afraid of Wehia's judgment. She hated herself for not telling Wehia the whole truth from the start: Lord Marik had promised patronage to the t'Tolani holding in exchange for Geri's hand in marriage.

"And this is why Aunt Hadana wanted you to accept?" asked Wehia. She had thought as much but had been reluctant to believe it. Was Hadana not a forge mistress of integrity? Wehia had heard stories of holdings falling into desperate times because they had run out of money. Was the t'Tolani facing this? A matrimonial connection with a powerful blood family would mean more business to the holding and the assurance of patronage. With the promise of such riches, the forge would be able to purchase more ore and other material needed to forge blades and weapons. And a blood family as in-laws would bring prestige and elevate the holding to an even higher standing in society.

Wehia was angry that Hadana t'Tolani would give away her niece just like that, for the sake of money. How could she be apprentice to such an avaricious woman? How could she make Fire Heart under this woman's tutelage?

Oh, Fire Heart, you might never be.

She would have to leave. Her mother would be disappointed, but she had to leave. And Geri . . . *Geri.*

Wehia would miss her room at the t'Tolani holding. How it had changed since she'd first arrived. It felt lived-in now: the walls covered with charcoal marks where she counted the days; gifts from Geri on the mantelpiece; piles of her work clothes; personal items strewn all over the bed.

The window was open, the nearby signal fire twinkling in the darkness. Somewhere, some woman was laughing. There was the sound of glass breaking. A man was scolding his child for being lazy and letting their stew go cold.

A soft knock broke Wehia's reverie.

"Wehia?" Geri whispered. "Wehia, are you there?"

"Yes. Come in."

Geri walked in, head bowed.

"Wehia," she said. "I am sorry. It's all my fault."

"It's over, Geri. There will be no formal proposal. No marriage. Don't think of it anymore."

"I shouldn't have—this shouldn't have happened! But what—what are you doing, Wehia? You're—"

"Yes. I have to leave." Wehia stuffed her clothes into her bag. She knew she was selfish and impulsive. Her heart burned hot. She did not like being lied to.

"No! Don't go. Please!"

"I am not sure I could make my sword under Hadana now."

Geri's face scrunched up as she tried not to cry, but tears spilled down her cheeks.

"You don't need to go. Lord Vess promised us patronage just today. Two years' worth of commissions. Just patronage. Nothing else. Don't go, Wehia . . . *please!*"

Lord Vess! At least he has honor, thought Wehia. Her heart broke to see Geri so sorrowful. "Oh, Geri, it is more than that. Aunt Hadana may be right—that I am not ready. I-I feel like I am standing on shifting sand. I should not be so easily distracted, yet clearly, I am."

"Wehia."

"Although how can I not stop and question what I have been taught when I find my teacher is a liar? When my dearest heart has hidden the truth from me? I have to leave. I cannot make my sword when I feel this way."

Geri hugged herself, crying softly, pitifully, hunched over. "I can't stop you from leaving, then? I hate myself for lying to you and not telling the truth from the beginning. I hated myself when I had said nothing."

Wehia threw down her bag and went to her amal, gathering the girl in her arms. "I know you are sorry. I am sorry too. I want to trust you again. I am . . . I am very angry at the moment. I trusted your aunt, Hadana. I called her 'Aunt' too. I just never expected her to be that . . . greedy."

Geri looked as if she had been punched in her gut. She shook her head slowly. "My aunt wants the holding to thrive. She cares for the forge."

"See, you're apologizing for her!" Wehia went back to packing. "Can you stop defending her? She wanted to give you away so that the holding would continue to prosper. I don't like that—I don't like that at all!"

"Oh, Wehia . . . I think you truly misunderstand her. She's my aunt . . . my mother's older sister. She's my only living kin. I love and admire her. She is family!"

"So, you see nothing wrong in what she expected of you? And you would have gone to Lord Marik willingly?"

"Wouldn't you have?" Geri said quietly. "If your family demanded it? Wouldn't you do the same for your family?"

"You don't even like him, Geri," Wehia snapped. "You would have betrayed your own heart and agreed to be his wife?" She yanked her bag's drawstring tight and hefted the bag on to her shoulder. She would walk all the way home, if she had to. She just had to follow the path of the River Verru and what signs there were. Her heart was heavy, a cold lump of confused emotions and self-righteousness.

Geri's face fell. Her lips trembled. "Will you leave? Were these months for naught?"

"I don't know, Geri. My heart is a mess." Wehia let the bag drop slowly to the floor. "I really don't know what to do next."

"I don't want you to go."

"Geri, don't."

"Don't go, Wehia. Don't."

Geri reached out, begging, and Wehia pulled the shivering girl into her embrace.

She realized that she was being rash. She was very much in the wrong too. Challenging a blood lord was a dangerous thing. She could have gotten herself killed, the t'Doniyat and t'Tolani holdings disgraced by her actions.

A scion from a minor swordsmith holding, challenging a blood lord to a duel: It was unheard of!

Swordsmith holdings were strictly forbidden to fight members of the blood families. It was stated in the law. She had indeed been foolhardy to challenge fate itself. The Sword Goddess had protected her this time. It was very fortunate that Lord Vess was an understanding and accommodating man. He was honorable too, promising the t'Tolani two years of patronage. Could she be like him? Honorable? Slow to anger? Back at her own holding, she'd often started fights, much to the grief of her mother and aunts. She was too impulsive, too headstrong. She had to be more careful, more mindful. Now, if she left, there would be much lost. Her mother often complained about the legendary t'Doniyat temper. Everybody in the holding had some of it, with some, like Wehia, more hotheaded than others.

"Must you fight everyone in the holding?" Wehia's mother used to scold, wringing her hands in exasperation. *"You are impossible! Curse your wretched temper!"*

Wehia remembered her sword mistress glancing at her ruefully when she'd become irritable during practice. Frustration at the inability to master certain sword drills had gotten the better of her, time and time again. When her heart had calmed, the old sword mistress would gently guide her through the steps again. It had been so simple. Why must she lose her temper?

And now, could her heart tolerate what Hadana t'Tolani had revealed about herself?

"My mother often reminded me to breathe when I felt anxious or angry. We forget to breathe when we let our moods overwhelm us," Geri said, her voice muffled in Wehia's shoulder.

Wehia and Geri held each other, breathing together slowly. That was what they could do. Heart to heart, they breathed, their foreheads pressed together.

Breathe. Heart. Breathe.

Listening to their hearts. Listening to their breathing.

Breathe. Heart. Breathe.

Outside, the vendors shouted to advertise their wares.

"Buy these waxed sausages, going at half price!"

"Have you bought your seeds for Shovel-tide yet? Come now and get them at the best price ever!"

"Hungry? My steamed peanut snacks will make you want more!"

It was another day in the City of Swords.

CHAPTER 13

IT WAS A COLD, subdued rainy night when Wehia crept out of her room and found herself wandering towards the dining hall. In the day, she had done her tasks halfheartedly. Hadana had stayed away from the forge, leaving the grim-faced Rika in charge again. The forge women had left Wehia alone, but their sideways glances and whispered conversations had felt like subtle jibes at her. They surely hated her now for what she had done to the forge mistress. She was the outsider who had caused Hadana's grief. The forge had felt damp and cold. Wehia hadn't stayed long. She'd fled from the place the moment her chores had been done.

She had no desire to look at her sword design still resting on her worktable. Her heart was truly a mess, a tangle of emotions, half-born hopes, and sharp agony. The mess had blocked the sword's song. She could hear it, but as if from a distance, as far away as the fens, blanketed by fog, a poignant and sweet fading voice.

One of the kitchen women took pity on Wehia and

poured her a large mug of sookee, the tree-nut-based beverage mixed with a dash of milk and a dollop of fresh cream. She also ladled a generous amount of morani stew into a big bowl, broke off a hunk of rye bread, and bade Wehia eat, lest she faint from hunger. Wehia was grateful for the kitchen woman's kindness. She stirred the pieces of meat and vegetables in the savory, brown broth and fed herself small spoonsful. The food warmed her stomach, but her heart remained lost and cold.

She had not left the t'Tolani holding . . . yet. Seeing Geri so distraught had frightened her. They had fallen asleep together, hand in hand, not daring to release one another, but when Wehia had finally woken up, she'd found Geri gone. After all, she had her own duties and responsibilities to tend to. In her room, suddenly isolated and alone, Wehia had not been sure if she would have the courage and strength to stay and work in the forge.

Her stomach grumbled loudly as she nibbled on the rye bread—and she had thought she would never feel hungry again! Like all the food in the holding, the bread was made fresh in the kitchen and the stew was rich and flavorful. She was soon cleaning the bowl with the last of the bread, letting it soak in the remnants of the stew. Perhaps if she fortified her belly, she would be able to think more clearly.

"Child? Wehia? It's not good to stay up too late and mope."

Rika stood at the door of the dining hall. She was still clad in her forge leathers. The women often joked that Rika never slept, so in love with the forge that she would stay up late to be in its warmth.

"Stop flagellating yourself with whips that are not even real," she continued, walking up to where Wehia was sitting at the apprentices' table. She smelled of linseed oil and other forge odors. She had been buffing and polishing scabbards for a display later in the eight-day. "My sister Hadana does not hate you, nor should you hate yourself. Mistakes are made. You should move on."

She said kindly, "Is your heart clear? No? Because, you cloud it with your own doubts. Holdings need to survive. We need to eat. So do the birds in the trees and the fish in the river. It is common, child, to make alliances with the blood families. Surely, your holding too survives on the goodwill of alliances."

"I . . ." Wehia was at a loss for words. Rika was right. Her head hurt. By the Sword Goddess, she really hurt, inside and out.

"Temper your heart." Rika's down-turned lips twitched, as if she smiled. "Go to sleep. The forge wakes early tomorrow. We have ceremonial swords to complete." Without a further word, the t'Tolani's second-in-command walked away from the table. Wehia could hear her singing a love ditty as she went up the spiral staircase.

Wehia was more confused than ever. Rika cared. She actually cared.

Could Wehia find it in her heart to forgive Hadana . . . and herself?

She retreated to the study with her sword design clutched tightly in her hands. It was a good place to hide.

A quick succession of knocks on the study room's closed door startled Wehia from her drowsiness. She had curled up in a chair, feeling sorry for herself. She was not sure why she'd wanted to be in the room, her sword design spread before her, the door closed to everybody else in the forge. She couldn't hear its song. In her current state, Wehia wanted no comfort. She was happy to wallow in her self-pity.

"Wehia." Hadana's voice was distinctive, even through the thickness of the door. "I want to talk to you."

The mistress of the t'Tolani holding looked as if she had not slept for days. Dark rings smudged her usually bright eyes. Her face appeared shrunken. Her fingers twitched nervously. Under the light of the study lamp, they were gnarled, like the brown roots of a tree. Hadana sat opposite Wehia—they were like two opponents in a qimaat competition, both not daring to move their pieces.

Hadana's fingers tapped the table's edge. She cleared her throat and spoke. "I am sorry I caused you agony. The alliance with Lord Marik was entirely pragmatic. I was thinking of the holding."

"Geri said . . ." Wehia struggled, feeling her throat seize up, as if filled with sand. "Geri said that Lord Vess would make a formal proposal as the head of his house, and that you would accept on her behalf because it would be a beneficial alliance."

Hadana shook her head slowly. "My niece spoke the truth. But . . . she never told me the extent of her distaste for Marik. Perhaps I heard what I wanted to hear, but to me, it was no more than a young woman's reluctance to leave her family home. Perhaps she was afraid of my reaction." She closed her eyes. "Yes, she was afraid of my reaction and rightly so. She loves the holding as much as I do. She wants to see the holding prosper. However, I should have questioned her more closely, found out what was in her heart. I thought only of the holding, not Geri's feelings. In my desire to safeguard the holding's future, I did not take Geri's wellbeing into consideration. I was too quick to believe Lord Marik's promises—it sounds like they were insincere and baseless. I should have spoken directly to Lord Vess. Yes . . . I was greedy. Geri's mother, my sister, would have been very disappointed with me . . ." Her voice trailed off.

Silence grew between the older woman and the girl. "Aunt." Wehia finally uttered the word, so fraught with emotion and meaning. "I apologize for . . . sneaking out of the holding to meet Lord Vess."

Sneaking out was what it had been. It had been a stupid idea, impulsive and stupid.

"You thought you would defend Geri's honor?" Hadana's smile was unexpectedly wry and kind. "Bloods do that. The swordsmith holdings used to. But it brought too much bloodshed and we stopped doing it. Only the bloods think it is all romantic and glorious to fight for your lover's honor or even duel for the sake of dueling, just to look good and to prove yourself right. Besides, it is now against Council law for us to duel with the blood."

Wehia stared at her sword design. She touched the lines with her fingers. The song was still indistinct. "I was being foolish. I am sorry, Aunt."

"We were both in the wrong," Hadana said, her voice still kind. "We both acted rashly. Our good intentions bore bad fruit. And so, I ask for your forgiveness." The older woman looked steadily at Wehia. "Will you forgive me?"

"Aunt, I—" Wehia's heart was a riot of emotions. Hadana apologizing to her?

"If I have made you more confused, I am sorry. I might not be the honorable forge mistress you thought I was. Once more, I ask for your forgiveness.

"Your heart is now a mess," she continued, her voice gentle. "You are torn. Your sword or . . . Geri."

Wehia looked up, startled, at Hadana, who nodded and smiled warmly. "You have made it clear how you feel about my niece."

"And—And you don't mind, Aunt?"

"Urban swordsmith holdings do not see barriers when it comes to love bonds, pairings, and unions. And if I had known, I would never have—well, perhaps I should have guessed, but, once again, I believe I only noticed what suited me . . ." Hadana smiled sadly, shaking her head.

"We—Geri and I, we are related, Aunt—"

"Oh, *pfft!* As far as I am concerned, the link has been so diluted, you two are virtually strangers. We say 'Cousin,' 'Aunt,' 'Niece,' but they are just words, at the end of the day. You can rest easy—I have no objections."

"Oh." Wehia didn't know what to feel. She was now a skein of confusion. She tried to calm the mess in her head. She had to be clear about this, for Goddess's sake!

"The crux of the matter still stands: Your sword or Geri? Can you have both? Are you able to focus on your sword and not let matters of the heart distract you any further? Holdings do whatever it takes to survive. I am sure your mother does it, only that you choose not to see it. That's the privilege you have been born into. The running of a holding, from top to bottom, isn't exactly pleasant, and it is downright cruel at times. Your mother has shielded you from most of it. You have lived a sheltered life, Wehia t'Doniyat."

Wehia remembered her mother, grim-faced on certain nights—were those times when there'd been no commissions and Rohana had worried how she would feed those under her care? Wehia recalled how she had, on occasion, asked her mother what was wrong, only to be waved away. Her mother would sometimes meet with the senior forge women, and they would talk, deep into the night, in whispers. Wehia had assumed it was smithing that was being discussed. In any case, Rohana's mood would invariably and eventually lighten and things would be back to normal. Until the next time.

"You need to decide, Wehia," Hadana said. "Are you strong enough? Will you disintegrate again at the slightest hint of trouble? Please think about this."

Wehia looked hard once more at the sword design, struggling to hear the voice of the sword. Its song was a muffled whisper.

Hadana stood up gracefully, placing her right hand on Wehia's arm. "I am sorry, Wehia. I hope you accept my apology, holding to holding, woman to woman. I am sincere when I say I hope to see the day when the t'Jirin swordsmith holding joins our ranks. You have the makings of a forge mistress—you only need to disentangle your heart."

"Aunt?"

"Disentangling sometimes takes a whole lifetime. Go to bed. I will see you at the forge tomorrow morning."

Wehia woke up early the next day and was already at the forge when Hadana switched on the lights and started the gears. The forge grumbled into life.

Seeing Wehia, Hadana t'Tolani smiled.

And so, at the start of the Hammer, Wehia plunged herself into sword-making. First, she went back to the sword design and listened hard for Fire Heart's voice. She looked hard within herself, within the messy swirl of emotions and desires. Buried under the tangled skein was the sword's song—Fire Heart's song.

Wehia was determined to make the sword. She'd spoken to Geri about this and the two girls had argued hard for many nights. Wehia's heart still felt raw and tender. She had struggled very hard to reconcile what had happened. Geri had apologized again about hiding things from her.

Would—*could* Wehia forgive her? Would she trust Geri ever again? Must Wehia choose between the sword and Geri?

"Do you need to choose?" Geri kept asking Wehia.

"Could you handle the sword *and* us?"

Wehia wanted to. Both mattered to her equally. Could her heart handle both? Both were equally demanding. Both required her heart to be strong. Could her heart be strong?

"I will try to be strong," said Wehia.

"I will help you," Geri said, reaching for Wehia's hands. "I am here if you want to talk. I will support you when you are tired. If you are hungry, I will give you bowls of morani stew and fresh rye bread. We will walk in the courtyard and count the stars. I can't promise I can always be with you—I also have duties of my own and errands to run. But I am here for you. Never forget that. Your turn." Geri smiled, lightening the mood.

"I will listen to you and your aunt," Wehia said. "I will not give in to my doubts and fears, and I will tell you if I am worried. I will also support you in what you do. I will hold you when you are tired. I will hold you when you are happy."

"Don't forget the stew and bread."

"I won't."

"Don't forget to breathe."

"I promise."

At the end of the discussion, Geri hugged her tightly, and Wehia's heart lightened as if metal weights had been removed from it. With Geri's support and love, she felt stronger. The skein began to break apart. When she looked at her drawing of once more, she heard it, loud and clear, the thin, singing-but-not-singing voice. Fire Heart's song rang forth in her mind, in her heart.

Wehia pored over the book of swords, researching steel alloys for Fire Heart. It had to be strong, its heart protected, and it deserved only the best materials.

The book included instructions for swords made from base metals and also a combination of base metals and metal alloys, like steel and bronze. However, no one made copper or even bronze weapons anymore. Such blades belonged to the past, when Metakse had been very young. Most of the swordsmith holdings used various kinds of steel alloys. The wealthier ones, like the t'Tolani, could afford to purchase the finest steel ingots, although they also made their own alloys. The blade must be perfectly balanced—flexible enough to withstand stress along its length, and yet hard and resilient enough not to crack or break. Blades had shattered before. Shattering blades pointed to poor skills and would bring shame to the forge woman and her holding.

Wehia decided that the sword's blade, her body, would be made from what was known as gem steel. The steel was made by smelting a variety of iron sand, found only on a specific part of Metakse's coastline, layered with charcoal in a purpose-built clay vessel, a tajam. The smelting took up to three days, during which the fire had to be carefully tended so that the heat was even and constant. At the end of three days, the tajam was broken and the block of steel plucked from the ashes.

It was a long and arduous process, and Wehia had to be focused and ready. Her heart and mind had to be resolute. Wehia was well aware of such demands on her. She strove to do her very best. She wrote down everything, making minute notes about every aspect of Fire Heart. Her diligence pleased the forge mistress and the forge women immensely.

Finally, kneeling, with her head bowed and clad in t'Tolani blue, Wehia accepted her tutelage under Hadana t'Tolani in a formal ceremony, attended by Rika and five trusted senior forge women. They waved Three Queens incense all over her, to bless and protect her from harm. The sword design was also blessed, with each of the women offering words of joy, because the making of a sword was a thing of immense felicity, perhaps second only to the birth of a girl child. After the ceremony, they had bowls of thin fen rice noodles served in hot, savory broth. Each bowl of noodles was topped with two hardboiled fen quail eggs. Gleaming like teardrop pearls, the eggs symbolized new beginnings and hope.

When the meal was done, Wehia was led around the forge, Rika and the senior women showing her the various stations and areas she would have to use when she began making her sword. She knew the forge, having worked in it for many months. The tour of the forge was another formal ritual, to show that, as an apprentice, she had access to all the stations and that for this part of her journey as an apprentice of the holding, the stations were hers. The forge women brought out their frame-drums and sang as they escorted Wehia around the forge. To Wehia's surprise, Rika sang with a sweet, clear voice. Wehia teared at the beauty of the song—it reminded of her own family's holding.

Her hair still perfumed by the incense's fragrance, Wehia was then given a ceremonial bath in flower-infused water so that she would emerge clean and pure for the making of the sword. They gave her new t'Tolani robes. Clad in her soft-blue garments, Wehia was welcomed by the forge women, and their urgently joyful drum bears more Three Queens incense. In the dining hall, where the entire holding celebrated with a feast, Wehia led the dance, holding Geri's hand. The women skipped and leaped as they danced out a Figure-Eight on the floor of the dining hall.

Wehia was feted with the best food and drink: the wine a fortified plum liqueur made by the t'Tolani and sold in the City to supplement their income, as well as the main dish, grilled ice-river fish, thick with milky-white roe in their bellies, and garnished with wedges of preserved lemons, their rinds sour-sweet to the tongue.

Wehia could not eat—she was so excited.

Then, in the silence of the night, when the festivities

had died down and the dishes cleared away by the kitchen women, the frame-drums kept in their goatskin bags, Wehia crept into Geri's bedroom for some quiet time with her amal. Standing by the window, they looked out into the night, over the rooftops of the city, at the flickering signal fires, and the Anvil and the Sword, bright in the sky. They held hands, listening to the holding while it breathed, listening to the City while the late-night vendors still cried out for business. They heard the distinct hoots of owls and other night-birds. For a moment, there was peace.

CHAPTER 14

The Month of the Hammer was a month of fixing, and a month of making. Swordsmith holdings and forges often received new commissions at this time, and this was also when it was customary to take stock of all equipment, repairing or replacing as needed.

And so began the making of Fire Heart.

As Wehia had made gem steel before, the complexities of the procedure were familiar to her. Nevertheless, it was a task that not only demanded her full concentration, but also required help from others. The sand and charcoal had to be heated at a constant temperature for three days running and this required the furnace to be watched at all times, and the flame had to be kept at just the right color and heat. Wehia had asked Rika and Geri to assist her, and they'd happily agreed. Shifts were worked out so that each could eat, rest, and sleep, with the tajam never left unsupervised.

At the end of the three days, the tajam was broken and Wehia triumphantly lifted out the craggy steel bloom produced by the three days' smelting. They were in one piece, but alloys of at least three degrees of hardness were produced, each kind gently broken off the bloom and separated according to type. The softest would be used for the sword's core, which needed to be flexible and springy so that it would not bend or snap.

The other alloys, including the hardest, were forged in alternating layers—heated, elongated, folded, and heated again, several times, to remove impurities, and then hammered into a long bar and bent around the softer piece of "core-steel." The two pieces were then forge-welded together and hammered into shape.

Hadana watched the drawing out of Fire Heart closely. The length of metal was, at first, nothing to look at, but Wehia held her sword's song in her mind and heart, weaving it into the metal she pounded at, flattening it into the basic shape Fire Heart would be.

Willing her heart clear of all distractions, Wehia focused on the blade, its length and its edge: It was hard work and Wehia's arms were soon screaming under the strain, her hands blistering, even though she wore thick protective gloves.

She tapered the blade, creating the tip and tang, hammering at an angle. The hammer beat as hard as her heart. She heated the blade, hammered, shaping the blade so it tapered to a point. The metal bulged, and she heated the blade again, hammering the thickness down.

Section by section, Wehia heated the length of metal she was working on until it was red hot, hammering one side of the blade, then the other, then back again, making sure both sides were equally worked.

Every now and then, Hadana urged her to heat the length of steel in the forge and then lift it out and leave it to cool down. Wehia gritted her teeth whenever this happened. She knew it was necessary to strengthen the steel, but the waiting caused her much agony.

Finally, when Wehia had hammered each section of the blade to her satisfaction, Hadana said, "Now, let it glow red hot, then bury it in sand and leave it. It needs to cool down slowly before the grinding and shaping begins." Wehia frowned, impatience burning in her breast.

"Perhaps this is a good time to think of making the hilt and pommel for your sword," continued Hadana.

Wehia had to dampen the surge of disappointment within her. She wanted to work on the blade.

"Don't let all this get into your head," Hadana said. "You need to protect the blade's heart. So far, you are not doing it."

Her aunt's comment startled her. What had gone wrong again? She was determined to seek the answer from Hadana.

"Aunt," she said timidly, "how do I protect the blade's heart?"

Hadana put down the brooch she was holding to smooth out the kinks of a dagger. The forge's sounds surrounded them, the sounds of a day's work. Evening was approaching. The smells of the kitchen wafted in. Forge women were tidying and cleaning the area. Wehia's stomach growled.

"How do you protect the blade's heart? By not rushing into everything!" Hadana said, this time with a hard edge in her voice. "You are too excited to see it done. Remember what I said before: You need to calm your own heart. Still your emotions."

"But I *am* focused!" Wehia protested.

"I noticed." The forge mistress nodded. "Wehia, listen to me. If you do not master your own heart, how do you protect the blade's heart? How are you going to be truly focused when you piece the sword together?"

Mouth open with surprise, Wehia reflexively placed her hand on her chest. She was tongue-tied. Hadana smiled kindly, as if to take the sting out of her words. "It's not only here"—she tapped a gentle finger on Wehia's chest—"it's also here." The forge mistress placed the finger on the top of Wehia's head. "Heart and head go together, just as the sword parts are part of a whole.

"Calm yourself, listen to your thoughts and feelings, remove the ones that clutter your heart," Hadana said. She went back to working on the dagger.

The forge mistress's words sounded mysterious,

almost magical. Wehia's own mother and aunts spoke of blade-making in similar ways. The making of a blade was a spiritual thing: the merging of mind and steel. Perhaps Hadana was right. She needed to master her heart. She had to control her emotions.

After dinner, she and Geri walked around the courtyard, holding hands and discussing their day. They stargazed for a while, then went to their separate rooms. Wehia fell asleep feeling loved.

Rika was assigned to help Wehia with the sword's pommel and handle. Rika was a good craftswoman and she approved Wehia's choice for the pommel—a simple silver alloy disk cut into a hexagonal shape, heavy enough to serve as balance and weight for the sword.

Rika supervised while Wehia worked on faceting the edges of the metal piece. The dour-faced second-in-command also showed Wehia the range of hard wood she could use for Fire Heart's hilt and went into a long lecture about why certain woods worked better than others. Oak was the best, followed by heart hickory. Rika droned on and on, and Wehia drifted off when the woman began advising her about the various benefits and drawbacks of using leather to wrap the handle.

Wehia chose a sturdy block of oak for the hilt. The uncarved and unpolished wood had hints of deep-brown whorls that marked the wood like its personal song. Would its song mesh with Fire Heart's song?

She began to carve the wood. When she carved, she sang.

> *Grow, my blade,*
> *grow, be sharp*
> *be keen,*
> *be strong.*

> *Sing thy song,*
> *sing it to the stars,*
> *Sing thy song,*
> *sing it to the skies.*
> *Sing.*

Images of home began to flow in her mind as she etched the details on the wood. The fen trees with their branches sparse, stark against a winter's morning. The ribbon of bright water swirling between her holding and the land. The call of the fen kingfisher, its plumage a flash of vivid sky blue as it darted from tree to water to hunt for fish. She carved a pattern of feathers, an arch of branches, and loops of river. When Wehia was done, even Hadana was pleased.

Soon it was time to grind and sharpen the blade.

Making sure that there was ample light, Wehia engraved a stylized snarling head of a dog on the unformed blade, then added the outspread wings of a crane, indicating her apprenticeship with the t'Tolani. When that was done, she began creating the edges for Fire Heart using a file. This work was relatively easier, as Wehia had done it this many times before at her holding. Up and down, up and down—Wehia watched her strokes as she moved the file along the blade's edges and tip. The edges were fine—even now, before the final polishing and sharpening, they shone brightly.

Fire Heart was taking shape before her and her heart swelled with tremendous joy.

She showed the blade to Hadana, who inspected it keenly, running a gloved finger along Fire Heart's edges. The forge mistress examined the blade for a long time. When her aunt finally nodded, Wehia heaved a sigh of relief.

Then came the hardening of the blade.

Wehia prepared a special mixture of clay, ashes, and polishing stone powder. She painted it on thickly to the center of the blade, leaving the edges exposed. Once the coat had dried, the blade was once more heated slowly until it glowed cherry red. Wehia turned the blade this way and that, ensuring it was equally heated along its length. Then, when she judged the piece was hot enough, she raised it from the forge and plunged it into a vat of oil. The uncovered edges of the blade cooled quickly, the steel hardening, while the center, protected by the clay mixture, cooled slowly, remaining springy and flexible.

That was, at least, the goal.

Next, the blade needed to be tempered. Once again, it was heated, although not to the same high level as before, and then allowed to cool in the air outside the forge. This heating-and-quenching process was repeated a few times. The aim was to soften the blade past the point of brittleness. It would be flexible, with its strength and sharpness retained and intact.

Once again, Wehia had to force herself to endure the lengthy procedure. Her face set in a frown, she marched up and down restlessly in the forge while waiting for the blade to cool.

Hadana cautioned her. "Why do you act like it is some sort of race? Enjoy the process. Pace yourself and be mindful of every step of the making. A sword is a precious thing and this is a sword that you are making for yourself. Cherish this time. It will not come again."

Wehia chafed under Hadana's words. The sword cried to her. The song soared in her head and made her giddy with its sheer joy. She wanted so much to hold Fire

Heart in her hands. She gritted her teeth, forcing herself to stay calm.

Fire Heart would be hers soon, she told herself.

So close, so close, so close . . . Wehia's heart thumped anxiously, eager to be done with the sword-making.

When Wehia wanted to make the cross guard, Hadana announced she needed rest. "A good forge woman rests when she needs to," she said. "You have the parts now. You are almost there. But you need to rest. Your heart needs its space."

So, Wehia spent more time with Geri. They held hands and enjoyed each other. She also practiced with Cold Steel, luxuriating in the sheer pleasure of drills and foot stances. She had been in the forge for too long. Practicing with her sword felt like what parched earth must have felt when the rain fell on it. She laughed, she sang, she danced with the sword. She felt refreshed. Geri watched her, clapping her hands with joy. Sometimes, Geri took out her dagger and they practiced together, exchanging tips on their different styles of combat. Wehia loved the way they moved, like dancers. When they were done with practice, they would watch the river hawks gliding on the thermals. It was breeding season for the hawks.

By now, the Stolati hummers were back in the courtyard, foraging and building more nests in the vines and nooks. The nests looked like tiny cups of dried vines and grass. The birds had even taken the thin brass and copper shavings from the forge, weaving them into the nests. They were works of art, and many forge women collected the empty old nests as talismans of hope and luck. Geri gave Wehia a nest; it was laced with copper shavings and resembled a delicate basket. The nest still had tufts of downy feathers at the bottom. It was very pretty. It rested on the mantelpiece above Wehia's bed in her corner room. She loved touching it. So fragile, but so strong too. Stolati hummers laid two or three eggs. The nests could bear the weight of the chicks and the parent birds. Would her heart, like a Stolati hummer nest, be able to bear all the weight of everything, her thoughts and her worries? Could she?

Even during the intense making of the sword's parts, Hadana had always made sure that Wehia had sufficient sleep. Each session at the forge would end promptly by the evening so that Wehia had time to bathe, eat, and sleep. Hadana was quite particular when it came to rest. "Don't you dare come back to the forge at night. The sword won't go anywhere. *Go. Eat. Rest.*"

Wehia's holiday was extended to the month of the

Sickle. Wehia slept, ate, practiced with her sword, and spent time with Geri. On the fifteenth day of the Sickle, she woke up feeling truly rested.

She wanted to go back to the forge and resume work on Fire Heart. She wanted to grind and shape the blade, to sharpen its tip and edges. Hadana was hesitant, for some reason.

"Rest more. We will begin in three days' time."

It was odd. She had never seen her aunt so distracted before. Not since after the incident with the Lords Vess and Marik. Rika was the one who told Wehia the reason for the forge mistress's lack of focus. Wehia was poring over the sword design when the senior forge woman stepped into the study without being asked. Normally, most forge women would knock or tap at the door's edge for attention.

"The fens are burning again," Rika said gently. "This time, more parts are on fire." Her expression was unusually kind.

Wehia stared at her stupidly before the realization hit her. It felt like an enormous blow to her chest and stomach. She couldn't breathe. "More fens are burning? Which part, Rika, which part?"

"The Middles."

The Middles! Home. *Home*, Wehia thought frantically, her mind suddenly blank, her heart gripped with enormous fear. This sounded more serious than before. The fires were much closer now. The Middles! Mother—her sisters—aunts—the ore dogs—the holding!

Had the border people done it? Had they set fire to the shrublands again?

"The border people—it must be their doing!" Wehia said angrily.

"Yes," Rika said, "always the border people's fault, eh? Don't be quick to judge."

Wehia blinked, confused at Rika's words. "What do you mean? They set fire to the Middles, where I live—my *home*!"

"So it is being said," said Rika, her tone vague.

"Why did Hadana keep this from me?"

"She wanted you focused, that is all."

"I have to go. My holding needs me," Wehia said. She left the study and raced up to the rooftop, her heart pounding furiously. Wehia yelled in anger when she saw the curtain of dark smoke in the distance. This time, the smoke filled one half of the sky. It felt like the entire Middles was burning. Why did the border people act this way? Her home was burning! *Her home.* Perhaps Mother was right, after all. These people were people with whom you could not reason.

She needed to find Hadana. She had tarried too long.

Her family needed her.

The sword's song was a dirge composed of silent sobbing and stifled screaming.

Wehia forced herself not to listen to the song.

CHAPTER 15

SHE REQUESTED LEAVE of Hadana t'Tolani so she could return to her holding. The forge mistress didn't object.

"May the Goddess watch over you." Hadana placed her hand on Wehia's head gently. In her rush to get home, Wehia forgot that she was ever angry with Hadana and was even glad for the forge mistress's blessing. "When you are done, come back."

Geri cried on her shoulder, but Wehia was resolute. Her holding needed her. She packed quickly. She ignored the Stolati hummer nest on her mantelpiece, all thoughts of fragility and strength forgotten.

Her half-formed sword remained in the forge. She would return, she promised silently. *Wait for me, wait for me. I will be back.*

With Cold Steel strapped to her back and a bag of sword-shaped coins for her journey home, a gift from Hadana, Wehia left the t'Tolani holding at the crack of dawn.

Wehia crossed the lake in a sturdy, steam-powered ferry, its hull cutting through the thin ice as if it were brittle Shovel-tide candy. The air stung her face; she had refused to wear a shawl or a face mask. She kept her eyes open for any sign of smoke, any sign of burning. And sure enough, there was a wall of black wood smoke reaching up to the sky. As Wehia watched, enraged, new columns of dark, billowing smoke emerged. Fires were being started even as the ferry sailed across the lake.

They were torching the swaths of forest!

The talk on the ferry had been all about the border people. Faithless border people.

"Vandals. Cruel. Selfish."

"Burning the forests. Burning people's homes."

"How cruel. How hateful."

"Let's teach them a lesson."

Wehia felt her hands clench into fists. She feared for the holding, for her mother's life. For her sisters and aunts. She was angry at the border people. How could they? Did the Middles deserve this? Did her family? Why? Enough was enough!

However, the memory of the border child surfaced, unbidden. Wehia bit her lip, her heart troubled.

A figure, wrapped in a head shawl and thick robes to fend off the chill, walked up to stand beside her. Wehia glanced at the gloved hands and at the distinctive curls of bright-brass hair peeking out from the shawl's edge.

"Geri?" Wehia gasped.

"I thought you shouldn't be alone for this journey." Geri's reply was muffled by the shawl, but her eyes sparkled merrily. "My aunt gave me her blessing. I did say I would support you, didn't I?"

Suddenly, Wehia no longer minded the thought of the long ferry ride. There was now Geri to be with—and to talk to. And talk they did, about everything and nothing. They bantered, sharing silly jokes and gossiping about the other t'Tolani apprentices and forge women; they discussed their hopes for the future, practical and impossible; they stood on the deck, holding hands as they watched the water and sky; they dozed fitfully, huddled together on a bench.

Wehia was anxious to be with her family at their holding and was grateful for Geri's company, but even the comforting presence of her dearest heart could not banish the worry that gnawed at her heart. The next fortnight that they must spend walking to the Middles stretched out interminably before her, but there was no avoiding it.

Every now and again, Wehia had to walk away from Geri and pace the deck, the walking seeming to blunt the sharp edge of anxiety. Near the end of the ride, they shared sookee sold for a few dagger-coins at the ferry's main deck. When the boat finally cut through the fog of smoke, Wehia realized they were about to dock at the jetty. She saw the familiar shape of the low buildings and the long bridge. The smoke was thick, with a hint of burned wood.

Wehia swallowed. Fear gripped her throat. Silently, she alighted from the ferry, Geri by her side.

They bought bread from a harried-looking woman who quickly turned away from them as if she were frightened of strangers. Wehia broke the small loaf in two and handed one half to Geri.

"What did Hadana say to you?" Wehia asked. "I can't believe she let you leave the holding just like that!"

"She simply told me to go." Geri coughed. "This bread is full of grit!"

After a day of walking, they rested at a small inn before setting off once more. Wehia felt a general unease in the air. Food stalls were closed early, turning customers away even while their noodles still simmered in hot broth. Women hushed their noisy children and ducked back into their houses. The minor swordsmith holdings they saw along the way had their shutters down, their doors bolted.

No smoke, either, from their forge chimneys. The somber atmosphere gave Wehia a queasy feeling in her stomach. She was glad for Cold Steel, strapped to her back, and was comforted to see that Geri had brought her dagger. It rested in its scabbard, hanging from her belt. Wehia had seen her fight with the dagger before, during the practice sessions with the apprentices and with her, during their quiet times together. Wehia admired her companion's ability to react quickly. She could defend herself if she needed to, being deadly fast with her blade.

The rest of the journey was, thankfully, as uneventful as Wehia's had been when she'd first set out for the City. What an age ago that seemed! This time, she avoided travelers' houses, sticking to inns. It meant paying more but was worth it for peace of mind. A spate of heavy summer rain, however, dampened Wehia's already low mood. It felt unseasonal, as if the fens had picked up her anxiety.

Delayed by the wet weather, Wehia and Geri finally reached the Middles after two eight-days—it felt longer! Things were decidedly grimmer here, the air so heavy with a thick haze that the two girls were forced to cover their faces. Their eyes smarted and teared, and everywhere they looked, they saw devastation. Burnt trees, whole swaths of forest gone, tracts of land blackened. Even the birds—the hawks and the kingfishers—seemed to have been driven away. The worst were the burnt houses, their rafters turned into charcoal by the fury of the flames. Livestock, gone. People gone, uprooted. Most had fled the Middles. Others who hadn't had perished. Unpleasant scenes were repeated everywhere they walked. They even had to avoid the burnt remains of human bodies and animal carcasses. Geri muttered prayers to the Sword Goddess for their souls.

It was obvious where the border people had camped and then moved on. There were patches of burnt grass where they had built fires; waste from the food they had cooked; wheel tracks and footprints in the dirt; a crudely carved wooden child's toy lying abandoned on the side of a path. Most striking were the sunbursts made out of straw and wire that hung from tree branches.

"Do they leave these to claim the land for themselves?" Geri mused, examining one of the sunbursts.

"I think I've seen these before." Wehia shivered at the memory of the thin, pale hand pressing a sunburst of straw and hair into her palm. "Beggars were selling these in the alleyways—in the City."

"You saw them?" Geri said.

"When I was out running an errand. A woman was

selling these, woven straw and hair," Wehia replied, recalling the disquiet she had felt.

"I've heard that the sunburst is a unifying symbol," Geri said. "Hey, wait for me!"

Wehia walked on grimly, the safety of her holding weighing heavily on her mind. The t'Doniyat holding was just down the road. Geri hurried to join her. The smell of smoke was pervasive. They felt like choking, the stench now also a permanent taste in their mouths. The outskirts were still smoldering. With her heart in her mouth, Wehia rounded the corner, expecting to find total destruction.

The white-stone walls still stood, their swordsmith sign unscathed by fire's touch. Even the small orchard where they got most of their fruit was green with leaves and emerging flower buds. The bog ran next to the holding's main building like a copper seam. Only the cornerstones of the holding showed signs of the fires, the bricks tinged dark brown. Relief rushed through Wehia when she heard the soft snuffling of cattle in the shed. They too had escaped.

There was the sound of a door banging open. Then barking, joyous barking. Two copper-colored ore dogs bounded towards them, their pink tongues lolling out of their tapered muzzles.

"Saki! Toma!" Wehia laughed as the ore dogs reached them, their tails wagging furiously. "You're so big now!"

Geri giggled as Saki, the larger of the two, stood up on her hind legs to plant a very wet kiss on Geri's face.

A robust figure ran towards them, clad in t'Doniyat colors of brown and red. She was crying happy tears, her arms wide open.

"Mother!" Wehia cried. The dogs barked, once, twice, milling about their legs. "Mother!"

Rohana t'Doniyat looked hard at her daughter. "You've lost weight," she said at last. Then she looked at Geri and smiled warmly. "You must be Hadana's niece. In a way, I am also your aunt. Come, come, let's not stand on ceremony—come in, rest. Let me prepare food and drink for you."

"Tell me about the burning," Wehia said urgently, her heart overflowing with things she wanted to tell her mother.

"After we have eaten," Rohana said, guiding Geri to the house.

"Mother—"

"Not now, my child. After the meal."

Wehia didn't like the tone of her mother's voice. She had heard it before. In fact, she had heard it countless times before, when times had been hard and they had lost patronage.

⊢——

They had food and drink—spicy mora paste, and fresh greens and herbs finely chopped and tossed in the same concoction, as well as mulled cider. Wehia found herself digging in, wolfing down the food. She was suddenly ravenous. She had missed the food so much! The flavors, the crunch of the vegetables combined with the hot mora, the sauces on her fingers.

Rohana wore a brown blouse, its edges finely embroidered with flowers and birds. Her skirt was a wrap with patterns of green and ochre swirls. She kept spooning more food onto Wehia's and Geri's plates. "Have more. You've hardly had any. You must try this. It was fresh-made today."

From where they sat, they could hear the sounds of the forge. Wehia found it comforting. At least the business was still busy. Life went on, even with the fires raging about them.

When they were done eating, Rohana sat them down by the hearth and told them about the burning. The ore dogs sprawled beside them, their ears alert, their eyes watchful.

"They came at night." Rohana's lips trembled, her anger barely controlled. "They came at night, skulking along the bog with their torches. I yelled at them, 'What are you doing?' They did not answer. They were as big as an army, but silent, oh, yes, like ghosts—hungry ghosts, all eternally voracious and cursed to wander the land. Then one of the women shouted back, 'You are with us.' I don't know what she meant. They began torching the forest. They razed everything. We were saved because of the bog. It is our border. It keeps us safe.

"By the Goddess, the smoke, the fire! The skies were dark with smoke, but the fire didn't come closer. Our neighbors didn't have our luck. Their homesteads burned to the ground. They sought refuge in the City and other parts of the fens. I saw them leave. A lifetime of work, gone, just like that! Nothing salvageable. The border people want the land for themselves. They are so angry. Treaties with them don't work. Talking to them doesn't work."

"But . . . is it true that some swordsmith holdings have kin among them?" asked Wehia. "Why did they join the border people, Mother?"

Rohana poured water into the ceramic cups. She sighed. "They are all outcasts. Some left the City and the fens willingly, for various reasons. Over the years, they have grown in numbers. They believe the land is theirs."

"I have heard they claim ownership with sunbursts," Geri said. "We saw the signs hung on tree branches."

"I have seen them," said Rohana. "They hang them on the branches of the border trees next to the bog. They believe that it is a universal symbol, since we share the same sun." Rohana pushed away her cup. "How is it possible to feel sympathy for their cause when they burn the land? It has happened for too long now. People have lost their homes and, many, their livelihoods. Some have lost their lives. The fen people cannot forgive them for what they have done."

Wehia and Geri felt heartsick at those words. What was the cause of the border people's discontent? There must have been a reason. Wehia frowned. What had the City done to these people? What was the source of their anger? She thought of the beggars huddling in the streets and alleyways.

"They sell the sunbursts in the City," she said, very softly.

"They wander the land," Rohana said. "Their suffering is no doubt unpleasant, but it is a choice they made. Why should we bear the brunt of their anger?" Saki whined and the forge mistress reached down to rub the ore dog reassuringly behind the ears.

"But . . . they want land, don't they? Why can't that be arranged?" Wehia asked. "Why can't the land be shared?"

"I cannot say," said Rohana shortly. "The treaties allow them to camp freely on empty fen land, but they have never honored their side of the agreement—"

"Which is?"

"Why, not to cross the border into the City. To live and let live in peace." Rohana snorted.

"But—"

"No, Wehia. Enough. We will talk more tomorrow, but now, I think it is time for bed. You are both tired."

In Wehia's old room, she and Geri heard the mournful howling of the ore dogs. Wehia imagined it was the border people crying—lost, desolate, and angry.

CHAPTER 16

ROHANA T'DONIYAT did not encourage more talk about the border people. Instead, she turned her attention to Wehia's half-made sword. She drew Wehia aside, into their study room, to speak with her privately. Why hadn't she stayed and finished the sword? Why had she left her task halfway? A forge woman was always focused and resolute.

"I was worried about you, Mother," Wehia said.

"You left your sword half-made," Rohana retorted. "That's unforgivable."

"Aunt Hadana gave me permission to leave. She understood. Our fens are burning, Mother. I feared for your life and the rest of the holding."

Rohana smiled briefly. "I am merely concerned for you. You wanted so much to make your sword, remember? It was your dream!"

"Aunt Hadana also said to protect my heart. It seems that is the hardest part."

Rohana's eyes widened at Wehia's reply. She chuckled. "She said the same to me—a long time ago. Your heart is the most important thing in this business, and rightly so. Go back to the City, Wehia. We will be fine."

Wehia gathered her mother into a tight embrace— she smelled of the bog, of the best earth. Of home. "Are you sure? Are you really sure?"

"Yes, my child. Now, go and help your aunt in the forge." Rohana's eyes gleamed with unshed tears. "Look after Geri. I saw how you looked at each other. I saw your rings. Take care of her and yourself. Please."

Wehia hugged her mother even harder, her heart overflowing with love and things she couldn't speak of. She still worried about her mother and her home. The border people were not going to go away. Their anger was growing. She wished she knew more about what lay at the core of their discontent. They did not have an easy life, of course—that was bad enough—but Wehia sensed there was more to their rebellion. She felt she must do something about it. At least try to find out more and see if she could help in any way. She could not just stand by and hope for the best. Could she? As for her sword . . . her mother was right—she must go back to the t'Tolani holding and finish making it. There was no question of that!

Rohana left the room and Wehia closed her eyes, inhaling deeply, calming herself. Yes! She would make the sword, Fire Heart, for herself *and* her holding.

Geri joined Wehia in the modest t'Doniyat forge. The forge women were making a shipment of kitchen knives for one of the City's finest inns. Wehia lost herself in the familiar work, listening to her aunts' and cousins' banter, helping them pack the completed knives in wooden boxes.

Wehia's old sword mistress dropped by, having heard that her student was visiting. She too had been lucky, her home untouched by the fires. Wehia enjoyed chatting with her teacher and they even found time to spar. Clad in her usual brown sparring leather, the woman showed Geri some moves, which the girl observed attentively, as if she were at a practice session with her own dagger instructor. Wehia was pleased to watch Geri perform the drills. She was such a quick learner.

"Don't forget to count from ten to one," the old sword mistress said to Wehia when they were about to leave the practice room.

"Ten to one?" Geri glanced at Wehia.

"It's an old calming technique," Wehia explained. "I

was very impatient when I was a child. I was a hothead."

"You still are," said Geri with a grin.

"I am learning!" Wehia countered, feeling defensive.

The sword mistress laughed. "Learn more quickly, Lady Wehia! Time will not wait for you."

Wehia later brought Geri to the riverbank where she had met the border child a long time ago. She told Geri about the incident. Speaking about it aloud lifted a weight off her chest. Geri listened without a word but looked on with kind eyes. The two stood holding hands as they stared out into the fen land.

In the evening, the forge threw Wehia a small party, a simple but delicious dinner to celebrate her home-coming. There was mora paste and the herb salad, as well as grilled fish liberally covered with ground spices. Wehia ate gratefully, touched by her kin's generosity. In the night, the women sang for her and Geri, wishing them well with blessings for their journey back to the City. Their songs were simpler than the t'Tolani's. Wehia sang too. This was her home. They were her family. Their drumming filled the night air and made the ore dogs howl mournfully.

When the drumming was done and everyone had

gone to bed, Rohana t'Doniyat gifted Geri an elegant dagger. Sharpened, it cut through paper.

"Protect yourself with this," she said. To Wehia, she simply said, "Look after yourself."

Wehia and Geri set off in the morning, their bags filled with grilled fish and two loaves of bread wrapped in paper. Rohana gave them a small pouch of dagger-coins, enough for at least two weeks of travel. Their bottles of water were filled to the brim, sufficient to last until they got to the first rest stop. Wehia bid her mother a tearful goodbye and kissed her kin, one by one. Her cousins wept and she promised to return. Wehia was touched by their tears. She then gave the ore dogs' ears a final scratch before walking down the path to the main road. The dogs' howls accompanied them and, even when they were too far away to hear the dogs, Wehia's tears continued to flow.

They saw more destruction and more of the sunbursts along the way, along the main road. The somber sights helped dry Wehia's tears but depressed her. Geri too was quiet and grave. They pressed on, stopping only to make quick work of the grilled fish for lunch. They approached the first rest stop near evening, refilled their bottles at the small well in the market square, and secured a bed at the inn. After a good night's rest, they continued on their way. This time, the weather remained fine and there were no delays; in fact, they were ahead of schedule, which pleased Wehia, who was anxious to return to the t'Tolani holding to finish making her sword.

However, it was not destined to be a smooth and peaceful journey for her. In the late afternoon of the thirteenth day, on the shrub- and tree-lined road to Fen Gorr, Wehia and Geri heard shouts and the approach of horses, so they ducked out of the way behind some thickly growing bushes, just in time to avoid a man being pursued on foot by three cloaked riders. The man was no match for their speed and the riders soon bore down on him.

Wild-eyed and dressed in rags, the man cowered to the ground, clutching a loaf of bread.

"You dare steal from us, you mongrel?!" one of the riders shouted.

The border guards wore navy uniforms with the insignia of the blood family they served emblazoned on their shoulders. Wehia and Geri recognized the insignia of the white lion rampant, partially covered by the soldiers' cloaks. It was the insignia of one of the City's blood families!

"My family is starving," pleaded the man. "Have some pity."

"Mongrel, your kind set fire to the fens and you dare

expect us to feed you?" snarled another rider. "You are worse than beggars! Filth!" The rider kicked his mount and the animal reared onto its hind legs. The man was knocked over, flat on his back. The other two men dismounted from their horses and began to beat the man. They laughed while they punched and kicked his face and stomach. The man cried out in pain, overpowered and unable to fight back. In the end, he curled up into a ball on the muddied ground.

Wehia and Geri shook with fear. Wehia felt something else: rage. Disappointment. And pain. Anger boiled in her. It burned in her chest. She leaped up. She wanted to save the man. Geri stayed her, yanking her arm with a glare. She would blow their cover.

The riders had their sport with the border man. One of them grabbed the bread, spitting in the man's face before mounting his animal. Laughing, they rode away. It was then that Wehia and Geri stepped out of their hiding place.

The man still lived but was bruised and bleeding. "Should we help him?" Geri's face was pale.

"He's injured!" Wehia said sternly and, with Geri's help, they pulled him off the road and lay him beside one of the bushes. They cleaned his wounds and bound his ribs with strips of cloth torn from their robes. The man struggled to speak, but Wehia hushed him. She reached inside her bag for some of their provisions. She gave the man a loaf of bread and a grilled fish. "For your family," she said.

The two girls then left, hurrying down the road, ignoring the man's grateful cries. They were afraid that the riders might return and listened fearfully for the sound of thundering hooves. When they turned back at some distance, the man was already gone.

Wehia had seen the soldiers' insignia before, on banners in the City. The soldiers must have been either garrisoned in the Middles or they had crossed the land past the farms. They were there as a police presence, to keep a constant watch over the fens and to prevent thievery. Yet they were behaving like tyrants. Did the blood families know what was happening? Did the blood families also cause dissent among the border people with their bullying and harassment? The very idea disturbed Wehia and she curbed the hot rush of anger in her chest.

When they arrived at Fen Gorr, shortly after sunset, she and Geri went to a small tavern, where they could have some food and drink and digest what they had witnessed while they waited for the midnight ferry.

Geri was trembling. "Will he be safe?" she asked plaintively. "Will he get home? Does he even have a home?"

"I hope so," Wehia whispered.

"What can we do, Wehia?" Geri asked helplessly. "What can we do?"

"I . . . I don't know," Wehia replied. "But there's

something not quite right. You saw the soldiers beating the man up, Geri. They took pleasure in what they did." She thought of the border people, of the sunbursts they hung on the trees. In her mind, the image of the man being trampled and abused by the blood family soldiers repeated itself and anger filled her heart once more.

Something had to be done. Surely, something had to be done. But what? And what could she do? She was just one person. Wehia frowned. Was she the only one who felt that things must change, that the border people deserved better? She shook her head, trying to calm her thoughts.

First, you have to make Fire Heart.

Yes, the sword was waiting for her. That was her first objective. She had made a promise to herself, and her holding. She had assured Hadana that she was ready and so she must see the making through.

Wehia turned to Geri, who was sitting quietly, her eyes closed. Geri was trying not to cry. Wehia gathered the girl into her arms. She had made a promise to Geri too.

On the ferry back to the City, when she and Geri finally saw the silhouette of the City's buildings approaching in the horizon, Wehia felt nothing of the awe that she had experienced when she had first made the trip. This time, the spires reminded her of grasping fingers. After disembarking, the two girls remained silent as they walked back through the winding lit streets. It was already late afternoon. Their hearts felt too full, too heavy.

When they returned to the t'Tolani holding, Hadana and the forge women welcomed them back with hot stew and oven-baked bread. Wehia and Geri spoke about the fires, Rohana, and nothing else. As if by silent mutual agreement, they didn't mention the man who had been brutally beaten. Geri went straight into her room after the meal. She said she was tired and needed sleep. Wehia left the dining hall shortly after, longing for a bath.

She soaked herself in her tub until her skin was wrinkly and the water was cool. Getting ready for bed after her bath, she found that someone had tidied her room, dusted the mantel, and made the bed with fresh, sweet-smelling sheets. Wehia sat in bed, hugging her knees. Try as she might, she still couldn't forget the face of the border man and the sunbursts hanging on the bare branches. These images had joined that of the child from so long ago.

Hungry, beaten, frightened wandering people. If they were so open to abuse, so abused, then no wonder they retaliated with violence. Outcasts, her mother had said. Why? What had made them so? And why had some from swordsmith families chosen to give up family, land, and steady employment to live with them? Wehia needed answers.

It was despicable how the border folk were harassed and bullied by soldiers from the blood families. Did the blood know this happened? Did they know and turn a blind eye? What could she do? Her resolve was slowly crystallizing and hardening. There was injustice that had to be . . . repaired? She knew she couldn't repair the problem the way she might with a broken dagger or a sword. She didn't think something like this could be mended easily. The problem loomed large and was intangible, unlike a blade. She couldn't hold it like a piece of iron ore or grasp it like the grip of a sword. She was only the daughter of a minor swordsmith holding. Ignorant in so many things, including this matter. She needed to educate herself. How could she help in any way unless she knew exactly what was going on? That was the first step . . . whom could she ask? Who would explain to her about the past and how it had caused the problems they now faced?

Wehia guessed that not many people knew much about the border people and their grievances. No one wanted to know. No one cared. She recalled her mother's furious words. Rohana had seen what had happened to their neighbors and friends. She would not be concerned about the border people's welfare. Others who had no direct contact with border folk were simply oblivious, apathetic. Most of the time, the City and fen folk let the

Council deal with such things. Let the politicians and councilors argue during Council. What did it matter what happened to the border people?

Wehia wondered if she was about to embark on an adventure that would ultimately prove fruitless. What if her mother was right, that the border people wouldn't even listen to reason? Even so, was force the only way to solve the problem? Look at what had happened to the man. It had not been force. It'd been sheer brutality. How could people be so sadistic and cruel?

Did she really want to go back to the fens again? What would *Hadana* say?

Would this plan work?

She inhaled deeply, remembering Geri's regular reminder to breathe, listening to her heart's rhythm. She wasn't . . . excited or anything. Her head was clear. She wasn't rushing into this. She was actually sitting down and thinking about this! Would she tell Geri that she wanted to go back to the fens? Wehia paused, shaking her head. Maybe she should. They always spoke about things openly. Geri didn't want a repeat of what had happened with the whole Lord Marik nonsense. Wehia bit her lower lip. She was thinking too much. She took another lungful of air and gathered it into herself, willing the clarity back. She needed to finish making her sword first. That was her primary goal, wasn't it? She'd traveled all the way from the fens to the City so that she could make a sword of her own.

Inhaling again, she vowed softly to herself: I will pour all my energies into making Fire Heart. I will hold the sword in my hands.

I will hold Fire Heart in my hands.

As for going back to the fens, she would have to wait until after her sword was completed. She gave herself some time to rest, to think about things, marshaling her energy and strength. She was strong. Like her great-grandmother. She could do it.

After Wehia had rested, her mind was clear again. She went back to her half-made sword, her heart more resolute than ever. She began to pour all her energy into making her sword. By then, it was the Month of the Scythe, and Wehia had spent more than two years at the t'Tolani swordsmith holding.

CHAPTER 17

WEHIA JIRIN T'DONIYAT *EF* T'TOLANI was on fire. She polished the grip of the half-formed sword until the whorls in the wood swirled in bright reddish brown, like the earth of her holding back in the fens. Then she tackled the making of the cross guard, ensuring that it was symmetrical and of the best steel. The forge resounded with the force of her mallet. The sparks flew; the metal glowed amber.

Hadana t'Tolani watched Wehia and wondered at the sudden passion she saw in the young woman. This version of her niece was markedly different from the young woman of just two months ago. This Wehia was focused, driven, resolute. These were qualities of a good forge woman.

When all the parts were assembled and arranged neatly on the worktable, Wehia was ready for the final making. She sang the song of joining, of the birth of the sword, of spirit and metal melding.

Wehia riveted the sword parts together, willing the

parts to unite into a harmonious whole. They were a precise and perfect fit. The song in her head grew loud and courageous.

"Make her sing," one woman cried out.

"Make her shine," another woman sang.

"Make her!" the forge women encouraged her.

In her mind, Wehia saw a fiery bird rise from the completed sword, its wings composed of the brightest and hottest of flames. It was the t'Tolani crane taking flight. As the bird rose higher, it became a hunting hound, long-limbed and tapered muzzle. It spiraled up into the starry skies, chasing invisible prey, its legs bounding with muscular strength. Like the fire bird, the body of the hound, too, was all fire. It was the melding of two holdings, the union of crane and hound, the merging of two schools of thought.

For a day and a night, Wehia sat before the whet-stone as it spun and spun, the sword's edges hissing as they kissed the stone. She sang as she made her sword sharp, until it keened with its own song . . .

Fire Heart.

Fire Heart.

Fire Heart.

At last, the sword's edges were sharpened. Hadana brought out a sheaf of reed paper. Wehia carefully traced the sword's edge on the paper. The parchment parted easily and the forge burst into more drumming and singing, the women celebrating the birth of a sword and the end of a long journey. For that day, all work at the forge ceased. Hadana declared it a holiday for the holding. Head tilted back, her voice lifted in devotion to the Sword Goddess, Wehia lifted the sword up to the light. She gleamed, the edges catching the light and looking as if fire danced along the blade. The balance felt right. The sword was whole and finally hers.

With solemn reverence, Wehia t'Doniyat slid the fully-formed blade into her scabbard. The forge women exploded into song. Wehia was led by the senior women around the forge, surrounded with the beats of drums and singing. She carried Fire Heart like a newborn. She watched as the women danced exuberantly. Her heart swelled with pride. When the dancing had died down, Hadana lifted a hand for silence.

"Who vouches for Wehia Jirin t'Doniyat *ef* t'Tolani?" she asked.

"I do," Rika replied, nodding at Wehia with a twinkle in her eye.

"I do." Geri smiled, winking at Wehia.

"We do," the forge women chorused.

"My kin have vouched for you," Hadana said. "Offer to the Sword Goddess incense and the best spices."

The forge women escorted her to the Sword Shrine, clad in t'Tolani blue. Their lanterns lit the way. Wehia sprinkled incense and spices before the impeccable statue of the Goddess and then held Fire Heart before her. She offered the blade to the Sword Goddess, singing the name of the sword so that She would watch over the sword and her wielder. Then, weaving through the crowd, the t'Tolani forge women danced their joy and accompanied Wehia back to the holding, where a celebratory feast awaited, complete with steamed fowl stuffed with the finest herbs; rich, spicy stews; and moon cookies and sweetened sookee for dessert. Before they ate, Hadana raised a hand, indicating that she would like to speak. She held a vermillion sash in her hands. Wehia's heart leaped at the sight.

"Well done." Hadana draped the sash across Wehia's shoulder. She was now a senior apprentice who could make blades and weaponry, under the supervision of a forge woman. Like Geri, who had made twin daggers of her own design, she still had some way to go before she became a qualified forge woman, but Wehia looked forward to the day they both reached that level. Perhaps they would start their own forge together.

"Well done."

"My profound gratitude," Wehia replied sincerely.

Geri kissed her on the cheek, beaming. "You did it!" she said.

They then feasted on the wonderful food. The moon cookies crumbled at the touch of Wehia's fingers. They were delicate and delicious. She licked the sugar off. Victory was sweet. She joined the rest in a circle dance, the joy swelling more with the drumming. Geri took her hand and they whirled around the dining hall, laughing. The t'Tolani celebrated.

Wehia stole away after the third long circle dance, which snaked around the hall. Fire Heart had been made. It was hers. Now she had other plans. Would they work? It was time to find out.

Geri, missing Wehia, went looking for her and found her in her room. She was packing.

"Where are you going? Why are you packing?" Geri demanded.

The feast had lasted into the night with more dancing. They could still hear the drumming in the hall.

"I must go back to the fens," Wehia said simply. She felt in her pocket and drew out a woven, silver ring that she had worked on at the forge. She pressed it into Geri's hand—her promise, her vow. Geri stared at the new ring, dumbfounded.

"But—why? Wehia, we have just come back from the fens!"

"I will leave at first light. I-I need to know more . . . about the border folk. I need to do what I can—to help—

if I can."

"The-The *border* people? Help *them?*" Geri repeated, staring in disbelief. "But—why—why *now?* And why have you said nothing before? We promised to tell each other everything!"

"I'm sorry. I meant to talk to you . . . Geri . . . do—do you remember what happened? The man? Beaten by soldiers? I do not think it was an isolated incident. The border people . . . I want to find out what they are facing. I want to know their grievances and understand what they are fighting for."

"Wehia, please *stop.* You are being silly. I am tired of all this running about. Are you being rash again? Stop being impulsive for *once.*"

"I believe, strongly, that the blood families are responsible for the whole mess . . . or at least, part of this mess."

Geri wavered, rubbing her face. She walked over to the window and stared out into the night. Finally, she turned to Wehia, her eyes shining with fierce determination. Wehia's heart leaped.

"I will go with you," Geri said simply. "You must not go alone. You must not leave me here. And I . . . I too want to know . . . the truth. I also saw the injustice, Wehia. It pains my heart every night when I try to sleep. I keep seeing the man and his injuries. I keep hearing the taunts of the soldiers. They are not the kind City folk I know.

They are horrible! I hate how they treated the man. But—"

"But what, Geri?" Wehia asked.

"It's not an easy problem to fix. We are not councilors. We are not even from the blood families. I think it is all far more complicated than we could ever imagine. Politics, Wehia. I am afraid. I am very afraid. We are wading into things we don't know anything about. And yet . . . I will join you."

"You don't have to, Geri. You can wait for me here. That is, if you want to."

"No. I made a promise to you that I would support you. I will follow you. But . . . But I will probably sit on you if you are ever stubborn—you know, counting from ten to one?"

"Oh, Geri! Will your aunt permit it?" A warm feeling suffused Wehia's being.

"She might give me her blessing. I don't know. She allowed me go with you to your holding. She might refuse this time. But we will ask her. Just promise me now that you won't leave without saying anything to me."

As a reply, Wehia t'Doniyat kissed Geri t'Tolani once more, on her lips.

CHAPTER 18

Wehia spoke to Hadana t'Tolani in the morning.

Surprisingly, she took the news well. With a mug of hot fen tea in her hands, the forge mistress sat quietly on her chair, listening to Wehia, who presented her thoughts clearly. The forge mistress was silent, listening, nodding every now and then.

"Wehia t'Doniyat *ef* t'Tolani, why do you want to find out about something that is beyond your control?" Hadana asked finally. "Your apprenticeship is going well and you have completed making your sword, as you wished to do. Why would you want to leave now, on this foolhardy quest? Think twice, Wehia. I had hoped you would stay and continue to learn so that when you return to your holding again, it will be as a fully-fledged forge woman. What would your mother say otherwise?

"Even if you wish to leave now on this fool's errand, you should not go before you make sure your sword is strong enough to withstand combat. Fire Heart is beautiful. But is it strong? You need to test your sword."

Hadana was right. Fire Heart was now a complete sword, but it hadn't gone through the various stress tests that working blades must be put through. Many of the forge women had offered to duel with Wehia informally so as to confirm Fire Heart's strength, and Wehia knew it was important to test her sword.

She steeled her heart. "I believe the border people have been wronged. I have seen how they are treated. It is wrong, Aunt, and you know it."

Hadana chuckled softly. "Of course it is wrong. There is injustice everywhere. In the City, in the fens. So, you want to leave for the fens? To do what? By going there, you think you can fix everything? Like you repair a blade? It is not just about forge-welding the pieces back together, my dear apprentice. So, Wehia, tell me, what do you plan to do? How are you going to go about it? Tell me. Plainly."

"I . . ." Wehia hesitated a little before straightening her back. "I want to find out more about the border people. I want to know everything about their situation. I want to know what made them choose the life they have now, and why some fen folk joined them. I want to know about their history with the blood families. Why do the blood seem to hate them so much? I want to know the reasons the border folk are angry. It is not just because they are suffering now—it goes much deeper than that and I believe that the blood families are mixed up in it.

And, Aunt, I-I believe my mother would be proud of me, whether or not I return a forge woman."

Hadana looked unconvinced. "The plan, as it is, is vague. I am not even sure if your mother would be proud of your decision. My cousin would surely object to your foolishness. Don't you think you are acting rashly, Wehia? Have you not learned from past mistakes? Do you even know how you will go about finding out what you want to know about the border people? Do you know how to find them?"

Wehia remained silent, her lips pressed firmly together. A tiny voice needled her: *Are you being rash? Are you?* She ignored it.

"I will . . . test Fire Heart to see if it's strong enough," Wehia said finally. "Then I will leave for the fens. I am sorry that my plan isn't clear enough for you, Aunt."

"So, I can't reason with you, and it seems that I can't stop you, either. I could simply forbid you from leaving, but . . . that is not my way. I will just have to permit you to go then," Hadana said wearily. She sounded sad. "You are probably the stubbornest apprentice I've ever encountered. Your head is harder than cast iron. It looks like your heart is firmly set on this as well. May this be a learning journey for you. Life is never easy nor simple.

"Hmm . . ." Hadana's eyes narrowed as she thought. Then she nodded and said, "I think you should lodge with the t'Nolyat. Their holding is close to your own—I am sure you have heard of them."

It was true that Wehia had heard about the t'Nolyat, but only that they were distant kin who shared a common ancestress with the t'Tolani, and that they kept to themselves.

"Why the t'Nolyat, Aunt Hadana?" she asked. "Why can't I stay at my own holding?"

"In the past, the t'Nolyat have had dealings with an encampment or two," Hadana replied and Wehia straightened, suddenly alert and curious. So, there *were* holdings who had interacted with the border people.

"And . . . I thought to spare your mother, my cousin, the worry of seeing you abandon your apprenticeship for the second time, although I confess, I do not like the secrecy."

"I see."

"So . . . I will send word to the t'Nolyat . . ."

"Thank you, Aunt Hadana. You have been most kind and patient with me. I am grateful." She then turned to leave, but Hadana stopped her.

"Hold, Wehia."

"Aunt Hadana?" Wehia thought Hadana might have changed her mind. The forge mistress looked as she did always: imperious, only a little sadder now, and tired. The young woman suddenly remembered the first time she had seen Hadana. It seemed a long time ago. Wehia was no longer the dust-covered girl standing before the great door of the t'Tolani.

"Remember, Wehia, keep your head and heart safe," the forge mistress said. "Think first before you act, my apprentice. Geri believes so much in you and I trust her judgment. Protect her and keep her from harm. Her life is in your hands. Promise me this is no fool's errand.

"You have so much potential, Wehia. It is raw, but there is much potential. Your heart isn't ready. Find your answers in the fens. The t'Nolyat are our kin. They will protect you."

"Yes, Aunt."

"May you grow from this experience," Hadana said solemnly. "I give you three months. Return to us when you are done. You have to come back in one piece to continue your apprenticeship."

"I will, Aunt."

Hadana's smile was kind. "I know you will," she said, finally. "Now, test your sword."

⊷╾

"My aunt gave us three months?" Geri asked incredulously when she finally met Wehia outside Hadana's study room. "*Three months?* What can we possibly do in three months?"

"I don't know," Wehia said. "Find out as much as we can? I still think Aunt Hadana doesn't fully believe in what I want to do. She does not want us to go."

Geri grimaced. "I am not surprised. Hadana is cautious . . . as *you* should be too."

"I now have to test my sword and make sure it doesn't break," Wehia said.

"Your sword has to be hardy enough to withstand combat," Geri said. "Maybe she also wants you to use this time of testing to think your plan through. It's not exactly the clearest of plans. Will the border people even want to speak to us?"

"She wants us to stay with the t'Nolyat."

Geri lifted an eyebrow, as if in surprise. "They are an odd clan. So secretive. They don't really talk much."

"They have contact with the border people."

Geri frowned. "Is that so?"

"That may be why they keep themselves apart. Or it may be that they are kept at arm's length by the other holdings. Why do some holdings and not others interact with the border people? You heard my mother speak about people leaving their homes to live with the border people . . . There must be a reason for that."

"I don't like that you can't tell your mother what you're doing. You will be so close to your holding and yet can say nothing. Oh, Wehia, there are things we do not totally comprehend. Some have tried to solve this rift with the border people, but to no avail."

"Yes, but . . . the t'Nolyat might have some answers for us. And we have three months! Come." Wehia tugged at Geri's hand. "We don't have time to waste! We have to test Fire Heart."

CHAPTER 19

Wehia kept her promise. She subjected Fire Heart to the series of stress tests agreed upon by all the swordsmith holdings to assess a sword's resilience.

Under the watchful eye of Hadana, Rika operated a hand-cranked contraption that tested the flexibility of the sword. Wehia cringed when Fire Heart creaked alarmingly. Her breath caught as the blade curved inward in the apparatus. Seeing that Fire Heart did not snap in two or break into pieces, Wehia's heart swelled with pride.

Next, she used her sword to cut through objects of varying degrees of density and hardness. First, she cut thick-skinned gourds and fruit, followed by wooden blocks and poles. Wehia was pleased that Fire Heart survived these assaults. The sword's edges did not chip, nor show any nicks. Even the finest fracture would have indicated failure. With a fracture, Fire Heart would be merely a decorative sword, pretty and useless like the ones hanging on the belts of fashionable lords and ladies. She hated the idea of having to start the process all over again. It would be humiliating to have to do that.

Hadana then insisted Wehia spar with her. Geri and the t'Tolani forge women gathered to watch the friendly duel, gasping and cheering as Hadana delivered hard blows, which Wehia countered successfully with Fire Heart. The sword held up well and Hadana then asked that Wehia spar with one of the forge women, and then another.

"I am still not sure about your sword," the forge mistress said darkly, even after Fire Heart had shown its durability during these clashes.

Wehia lifted Fire Heart to the light. "There are no faults, no cracks, Aunt. I think she is fine."

Despite Hadana's misgivings, the sword parts remained firm. During her sparring sessions, Wehia had listened closely in order to catch any worrisome sound from Fire Heart. For example, a loose cross-guard would rattle. The sound could also mean the tang wasn't joined properly. At her holding, she had heard badly made knives rattle. Such sounds signified poor workmanship. Any self-respecting forge woman would have been embarrassed. Ashamed.

Hadana insisted on more tests to prove the sword's

strength and resilience. She had Wehia tightly roll rice straw mats and then soak them with water to increase their density. Wehia had to use Fire Heart to slice through these mats at different angles.

"It is as close as you will get to flesh," Hadana said dryly, adding that the lengths of green xylia stalks she had lined up for cutting would give Wehia a good idea of what it was to cut through bone.

Subsequently, Wehia used Fire Heart to thrust and cut through metal plates and pieces of tough leather. She performed these actions while standing still and also stepping towards her target.

Fire Heart held up beautifully. Wehia was filled with pride and delight, but Hadana merely observed with a thoughtful expression. However, Wehia was impatient to leave the t'Tolani holding.

After another vigorous duel with Hadana, Wehia returned to her room, wiping her perspiration. A warm glow of satisfaction suffused her. Fire Heart had held up. She was successful. She could finally leave the t'Tolani holding.

She slid Fire Heart from its scabbard to admire it under the light. It was gorgeous. Turning the sword this way and that, Wehia marveled at its graceful lines. It was beautiful . . . She ran a finger up the center of the blade and—No! Wehia's finger froze. She took a closer look and . . . it was as if her entire body had been plunged into freezing water.

Her heart crumbled: There, right in the middle of the cross-guard, where it joined with the blade, was a tiny hairline fracture—tiny enough to be missed if you were not looking hard.

Wehia tried rubbing off the crack—it was fine, so fine, like a strand of hair. It might just have been some blemish . . .

It wouldn't come off, no matter how hard she rubbed.

No . . .

Wehia sank onto her bed. The room spun. She tasted bitterness in her mouth. She doubled over, retching. Shame and embarrassment engulfed her. And disappointment. Why, why, why? Why was it only now that the fracture showed? Hadana was right, after all. Wehia hadn't been ready. She had rushed into Fire Heart's making and she had rushed the making itself. She had been conceited. And wrong. Wrong. So wrong.

Wehia blinked back hot tears. She had to hide this from Hadana. From Geri. From everyone. *Mother*, she thought, sick to her stomach. Perhaps running away to the t'Nolyat was the answer.

She wanted to hide from Hadana's sharp tongue and eyes. She had failed her teacher. And her holding.

And herself.

She wanted to run away.

There was one final test involving cutting and slicing with the sword. Hadana wanted Wehia to repeat the test, using animal carcasses.

"We used the mats and the xylia stalks, but there is nothing like real flesh and bone," said Hadana.

Wehia shook. She was afraid. What if the fracture widened? What if Fire Heart broke, revealing her failure?

But Fire Heart sliced easily through the boar carcass and its edge remained sharp, keen. Wehia breathed a shallow sigh, afraid that Hadana and the forge women could hear her heart beating loudly in her chest.

"The sword cuts well," observed Hadana solemnly. "I am proud of your work, Wehia. I am proud of you."

Wehia nodded mutely, wiping Fire Heart's blade before sliding the sword into her scabbard. She dreaded Hadana's judging eyes, terrified that the woman might catch a glimpse of the fracture.

But it is so small, Wehia argued with herself. *She won't see it. She won't see it at all.*

"You look pale," Hadana continued. Wehia bit her lower lip. *Please, please, please, stop.* "Are you well, Wehia?"

"I am well," Wehia quickly replied. She held Fire Heart close to her. *Please, please, please stop asking me questions.*

"I am pleased that Fire Heart is a success. It is a good sword."

Wehia bowed her head, as if she agreed with Hadana's statement. Inside, raw emotions swirled. She tried hard to stop herself from crying. She was not worthy of Hadana's praise.

Presently, when she checked Fire Heart secretly in her room, away from the prying eyes of the forge—away from *Hadana*—Wehia found that the fracture was still there. She had hoped that she would find it gone, miraculously vanished, thanks to her prayers, but it was there. It hadn't grown longer or wider. Nor was there the telltale spider webbing of fractures that would have meant that Fire Heart was indeed breaking apart.

The fracture mocked her. It exposed her for what she was. A fake. A liar.

Liar.

The crack in Fire Heart reminded her of her guilt. Her *failure*.

Wehia was relieved that there were no more tests to carry out. She waited in dread for Hadana t'Tolani to summon her and question her further, but the forge mistress did not do so. Hadana informed Wehia that she had sent word via messenger on horseback to the t'Nolyat explaining Wehia and Geri's arrival.

Before Wehia was due to leave, the t'Tolani forge women took her and Geri to the Shrine to offer trinkets and prayers for safe travel.

Wehia prayed for protection and wondered if the Goddess was testing her resolve. Geri placed a garland of steel flowers at the statue's feet, whispering a few prayers before blessing herself with the holy water held in the font next to the Goddess.

Standing there, before the statue of the Goddess, Wehia felt exposed and ashamed. Surely, *She* could see Wehia's folly. Surely, *She* knew about the fault in Fire Heart.

"Are you feeling faint?" whispered Geri. "You look so pale."

Wehia shook her head. "It's just so hot," she lied. "I'm fine." She had promised to always speak the truth to Geri, but she was hesitant. Afraid. She hated herself for keeping this secret, but she just couldn't tell her amal about Fire Heart.

When the t'Tolani women returned home, they

proceeded to the dining hall. There had been planned a modest farewell supper for Wehia and Geri. The dishes were simple: grilled dumplings filled with chopped chives and minced fowl, as well as platters of sliced cold meat from their larder. Instead of wine, there was only fresh, cold water. Even the normally loud drums were silent. There was no singing, no laughter.

When the meal was done, the forge women came over to Wehia and embraced her. They gave her words of encouragement. Some gave her talismans of protection, shaped like small knives, and small, velvet bags filled with dagger coins.

"We will see you again after three months or so," Rika said, hugging Wehia and Geri. "Find out what you can. Go with the Goddess."

When it came to Hadana's turn to give them her blessings, she whispered in Wehia's ear, "May the Sword Goddess look after you." She then kissed Wehia on the cheek and gifted her with a back sword strap that she had made herself. Dark brown and soft to the touch, it smelled of the finest leather and warm seed oil.

Wehia cringed inwardly, thinking of the fine crack on Fire Heart. She was touched by the kindness shown by everyone but was also secretly relieved that she wouldn't see them for a while.

The next day, when the sun's rays had turned the roof

of the basilica golden, Wehia strapped on her swords—Cold Steel by her side, Fire Heart on her back—shouldered her bag, and, with Geri by her side, left the t'Tolani holding.

A final look back afforded Wehia Jirin t'Doniyat *ef* t'Tolani the sight of Hadana t'Tolani, standing at her door, a tall, proud figure in blue, her hand lifted in farewell.

METAKSE, A GUIDE

APPRENTICE

An apprentice trains under an experienced forge woman, often the forge mistress herself. They run errands and do the more menial tasks at the forge. An older apprentice seeking the rank of forge women would intend to make a weapon of her choice. Attainment of this rank (also applies to senior apprentices) is marked with riotous celebrations and food in the form of noodles with two eggs to symbolize fruitfulness. It varies, from holding to holding and at the discretion of the forge mistress, how apprentices are elevated to senior apprentices and forge women. Some senior apprentices serve as forge women in holdings that might require their assistance.

AMAL

A term of affection between two people. It means "dearest heart" or "love".

BARETTI PARROTS

Parrots known for their colorful plumage and loud squawking. They are popular as pets.

BOOK OF SWORDS

An important record kept by swordsmith archivists to keep track of the styles and kinds of blades and weapons made by the holding. A holding's book of swords records both its history and lineage.

<table>
<tr><td>BORDER
PEOPLE</td><td>Largely nomadic and itinerant groups of people. They often include individuals affected by poverty and loss. They literally live along the border between the fens and the sea. The City of Swords perceives the border people as ruffians and thieves.</td></tr>
<tr><td>BLOOD</td><td>The aristocratic families in the City of Swords are often called the blood or the blood families. They are members of the Council, which controls the political and economic interests of the land, holding frequent meetings and debates to decide on important matters of state. Certain blood families hold military power and organize the regiments who patrol the land.</td></tr>
<tr><td>CIDER</td><td>Often drunk warm during the winter months. It is made with either apples or pears.</td></tr>
<tr><td>DAGGER-COIN</td><td>A type of money used in Metakse. One dagger-coin is approximately worth one Metaksean dollar.</td></tr>
<tr><td>DOMMET
DRUMS</td><td>Light frame drums used by women in the swordsmith holdings. They are played during celebrations and festivals. The size of the drums vary. The ones used by the t'Doniyat are the size of handheld rice sifters.</td></tr>
</table>

FAMILIAL TERMS	**t':** prefix for clan. It means "the clan of . . ." **ef:** This suffix, placed after the names of an adopted female child or an apprentice, and before the clan name the child has joined. It means "belonging to . . ." For example, Wehia Jirin t'Doniyat *ef* t'Tolani and Geri Shaara *ef* t'Tolani. *Every girl child from the swordsmith holdings is given two names at birth. Her second name will be the name of her own household or holding, with its own forge. For example, if Wehia has her own holding, it will be called the t'Jirin holding and Wehia will then be called Wehia t'Jirin.*
FEN	Or fens. The moor-like wide spaces, with straggly groves and frequently flooded and misty. The area south of the City is considered largely problematic with constant uprisings by the border people.
FEN PONY	A type of wild pony found in the fens. They are often domesticated for riding and to carry luggage. Fen ponies have thick brown or dun-colored coats that grow shaggy during winter.
ICE FISH	A fish species that live in the Verru river and thrive under ice. Their meat is thick and sweet.

INKS	Apart from its swords, Metakse is also famous for the inks produced by families who specialize in ink and dye production. The inks and dyes, made from plants from the outer islands, are highly pigmented, expensive but of excellent quality. Many swordsmith holdings use such inks for their books of swords. Examples of these inks are Verusian black and Jessian silver.
JESSIAN	The name of a special silver-hued ink derived from jess, a kind of plant found on the outer islands. The plant's stems produce the distinctive silver color beloved by inkmakers and swordsmith holding archivists. The stem of the jess plant is also mildly toxic and must be harvested while wearing thick gloves.
LANGUAGE	The people of Metakse speak a common tongue, called Askan, which means 'language'.
MORA PASTE	Also called 'mora', this is a reddish spicy paste eaten with food. Each family has their own recipe for the paste.
MORANI STEW	Eaten all year around, this is a soupy stew made with meat, vegetables and tubers, and is best eaten with hot bread or river rice. Each family has their own version.

MOON
COOKIES

A delicious sweet treat and dessert. Crescent-shaped, they are feather-light and dusted with powdery sugar.

PROMISE
RINGS

Given to a loved one. They are not betrothal rings.

QIMAAT

A board game, rather like chess, played by two people.

RACE

Metakse is monoethnic, but not mono-cultural, as regional variations have developed in food, music, dress and other customs and practices.

RELIGION

The Sword Goddess is worshiped in her Shrine in the City of Swords. She is the patron of young lovers, young women and swordsmiths, but all seek her protection.

The Goddess's feast days occur in the months of the Shovel, the Flint, and the Saber.

Offerings include white candles, small swords, daggers, ores, shovels, and tiny trinkets made of steel and silver.

RIVER RICE

A type of grain growing wild in rivers and streams. It is also cultivated commercially.

SHOVEL-TIDE

New year celebrations. It is celebrated with gift-giving. Popular gifts are necklaces and bracelets, and other trinkets.

SOOKEE	Popular beverage made from nuts. Thick and sweet, it is drunk topped with fresh whipped cream as a treat. It is also drunk as a breakfast drink. Some people prefer it unsweetened.
SIGNAL FIRE	Maintained by women trained with knowledge of chemistry, the signal fire burns constantly like a beacon at the top of the main building of a holding. Different colors symbolize different things. Blue means that a message is on its way; green stands for peace; red, danger.
STEAM	Most of the holdings and the aristocratic blood families run on steam. Steam generates energy for amenities like hot water, heat and lighting. Councilors have debated the use of steam as burning of coal pollutes the air.
STOLATI HUMMERS	Tiny birds that resemble hummingbirds. They feed on flower nectar and make tiny cup-like nests. Their feathers shimmer in metallic tones.
SUNBURST	A sun-shaped talisman made with dry brush, wires or hair.
SWORDSMITH HOLDING	Matriarchal and matrilineal clan born and trained to make specific or specialized blades or steel objects. The skills are passed from mother to daughter or from aunt to niece.

TAJAM	Furnace used in the making of gem steel.
TOFFEE FRUIT	Fruits dipped in toffee, a street food sold in the City throughout the Metakse year. The overall texture is crunchy on the outside and soft inside.
VERRU (RIVER)	An important river that runs through and bisects the City of Swords. Deep and dark-colored (because of black silt), this river serves as a transportation route and a vital source of food and water. It ends at a delta close to the southeast coast.
VERU	A plant, found in the outer islands, used to make the famous Verusian Black ink. The name comes from the word "ver", which means black or dark.
WRAP	Worn by the women in some swordsmith holdings. The t'Doniyat are known to wear distinctive wraps of dyed textiles woven with vivid patterns.
WEEKS & DAYS	A week comprises eight days and is called an eight-day. The days do not have names and are simply referred to as First, Second, Third, etc.

XYLIA

A type of plant found in some parts of the colder fen regions closer to the mountain ridges. It is actually a type of grass with a shiny but resilient "bark" and hollow stem. Used by the mountain people as food and kitchenware. Also used by the swordsmith holdings to test their blades. Pronounced SEE-lia.

MONTHS OF THE METAKSE YEAR

SHOVEL — The first month of spring. Celebration of spring. Shovel-tide marks the celebration of spring.

HAMMER — Mid-spring. Families commission weapons as gifts or for their own use. People use this time to do repairs of houses and holdings.

SICKLE — The last month of spring. Novice-taking takes place during this month. Early produce is harvested.

DAGGER — The first month of summer. Harvesting begins. City folk begin celebration of marriages and parties.

AXE — Mid-summer. Harvesting. Skinning of livestock. Celebration of marriages and parties.

SCYTHE — The last month of summer. Harvesting and skinning continues. Waxing of meats and making of sausages begin. The number of commissions traditionally drops around this period, though City and fen holdings are kept busy with two or three medium-to-big projects normally commissioned by wealthy families.

FLINT   The first month of autumn. The Feast of the
                     Flint. People celebrate with sausages. Farmers
                     begin weaning the young of their livestock.
                     Sausages and waxed meats are stored in
                     preparation for the winter months. Birds and
                     animals begin fattening up and start their
                     hibernation. Nest-building slows down and
                     stops. Farmers till and plow their fields.

HOOK   Mid-autumn. Farmers begin to house their
                     animals indoors in preparation for winter.
                     Repair of heaters. Stocking up on wood and
                     coal.

SWORD   The last month of autumn. Farmers sell rams
                     and other male livestock at the markets.

KNIFE   First month of winter. Forge women do their
                     stock-taking and inventory. Last-minute
                     commissions are completed. Around this time,
                     the holdings stop taking in commissions.

SABER   Mid-winter. Stock-taking. Hummers hibernate.
                     Plants are more or less bare.

PLOW   The last month of winter. Month of planning
                     for the coming year. Winter plowing continues.

ABOUT THE AUTHOR

Joyce Ch'ng lives in Singapore. They write science fiction and fantasy as well as YA and MG. Their short stories have appeared in *The Apex Book of World SF II*, *The Future Fire* and *Multispecies Cities*. *Dragon Dancer* (Lantana Publishing) is Joyce's first picture book, celebrating dragon dancing and Lunar New Year; it was followed by *Oyster Girl* (Pepper Dog Press), a tribute to their grandmother and the hawker heritage in Singapore. For YA readers, *Fire Heart* is a fantasy book about swords and coming-of-age. You can find Joyce at their website (awolfstale.wordpress.com), or on X and Bluesky at @jolantru.